HAL SMALL

AN UNADJUSTEDS STORY

MARISA NOELLE

The Shadow Keepers

The Unraveling of Luna Forester

Plastic

The Mermaid Chronicles Series

Secrets of the Deep

Quest for Atlantis

Fight for Freedom

Ghost Pirates

Vendetta

Denizens of Darkness

Vortex Returns

The Mermaid Chronicles Companion Guide

This book contains themes and references that some readers may find distressing, including, but not limited to:

Violence – Physical fights, gunfire, and injury.

Death – Loss of loved ones, including a child, depicted in emotionally intense ways.

Torture/Abuse – Government brutality, forced enhancement, and systemic mistreatment.

Oppression – Totalitarian control, discrimination against the unenhanced, and loss of bodily autonomy.

Rebellion/Anarchy – Acts of resistance, sabotage, and organized uprising.

Imprisonment/Enslavement – Forced detention and threat of execution.

Manipulation/Brainwashing – State propaganda and coercive enhancement mandates.

Mental Health Issues – Grief, PTSD, depression, and survivor's guilt.

Prejudice – LGBTQ+ persecution mentioned in past protests.

Body Horror/Mutations – Genetic enhancements, augmentation malfunctions, and physical deterioration.

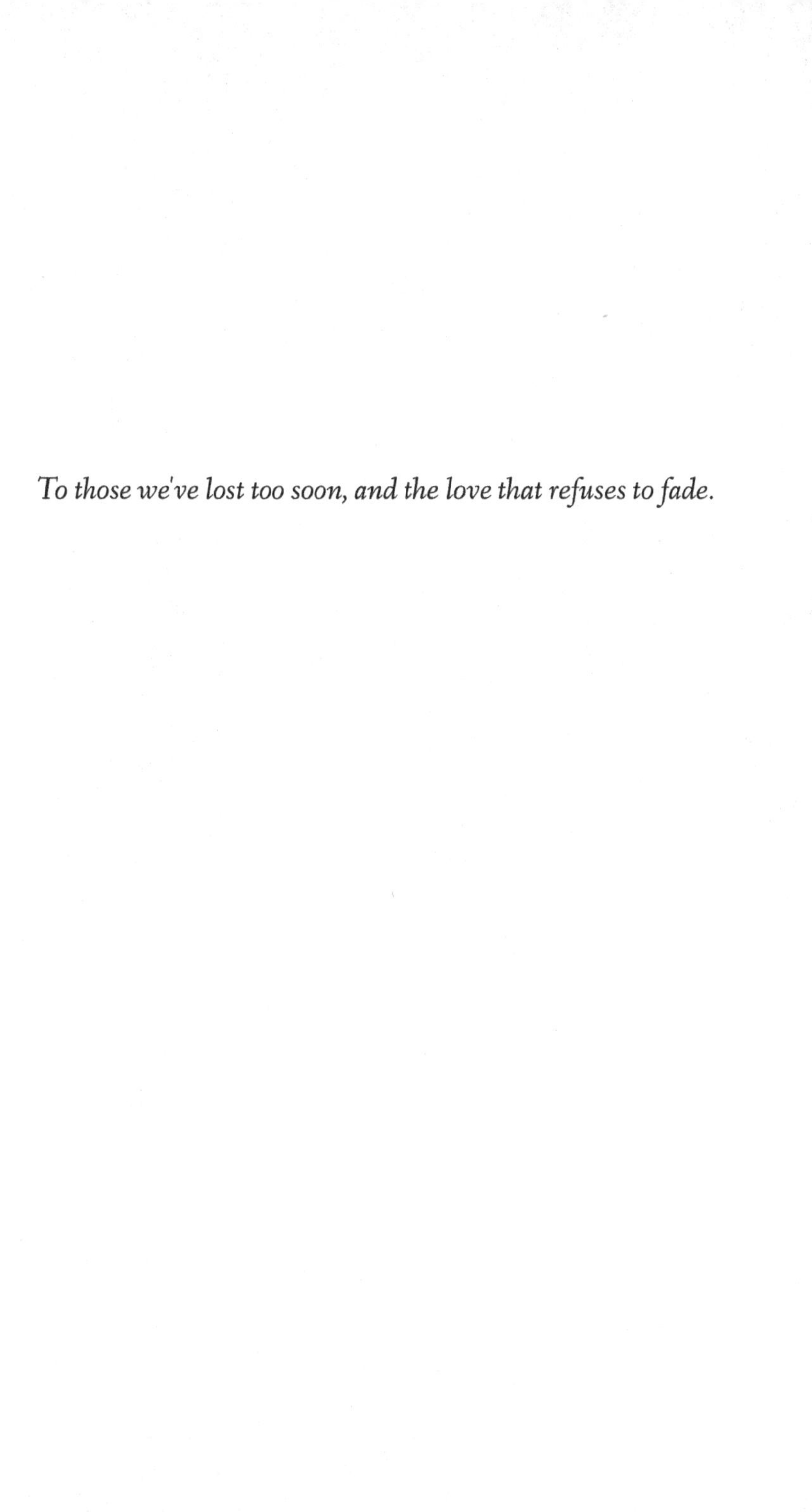

To those we've lost too soon, and the love that refuses to fade.

CHAPTER 1

Hal's future is waiting.

It's all right in front of him. He just has to grab it. If he plays well, that four-year contract with unlimited regeneration nanites will be his. Maybe a shoe or a drink commercial too. He'd love to snag a deal with BioBurst, because not only does it boost performance, it actually tastes good too.

Adrenaline courses through his veins as Hal scans the field. It's a familiar companion. One he relishes. The roar of the crowd swells around the stadium, sixty thousand voices melding into a single entity hungry for the spectacle of enhanced bodies colliding at superhuman speeds. Hal adjusts his helmet, his body humming with energy, ready to run and dive and smash his opponents.

He still marvels at the strength in his body, the gifts the nanite gave him. It's been nearly ten years since he took the bulk nanite, but every night he thanks his lucky stars.

"Ready to crush it, Small?" Coach Decker slaps Hal's

shoulder pad, his weathered face creasing into what passes for a smile.

"You bet." And he is. Because he's playing on his home ground. The field he's come to love over the last seven years is his second home. His team? The Central City Reapers. Two Super Bowl wins. It doesn't get much better than that.

The tunnel vibrates with the stomping of feet above, the crowd growing impatient. Hal breathes in the recycled air, tinged with the smell of industrial cleaner and sweat. Beside him, the other players paw at the ground like racehorses straining to be released. Only three players on their team remain unadjusted—Miller, Jackson, and Ramirez—scattered like dandelions among a field of steel. Their bodies are noticeably leaner, their eyes a touch more anxious. There's a fragility to them that the nanite-enhanced players don't possess, a reminder of human limitations in a sport that increasingly demands more than humanity was designed to give.

"Let's make them work for their paychecks today," Dominguez murmurs, the team's star receiver, nodding toward the Baltimore Barons waiting at the other end of the field. His skin shimmers with a faint copper glow—an unnecessary cosmetic addition to his class-8 reflex enhancement, but one that makes him instantly recognizable to fans and merchandise buyers. And boy, does he rake in the money with his royalties.

The signal comes, and they burst from the tunnel into blinding light. The crowd explodes, the sound physical enough to push against Hal's chest. He raises a hand, acknowledging their cheers, using their energy to fuel his determination.

The field stretches before them, impossibly green and perfect. Hal's cleats bite into the turf as they warm up, his muscles loosening with each practiced movement. Across the field, the Barons' defensive line looks formidable—all bulk-enhanced, their shoulders broad, necks thick as tree trunks. Hal spots only one unadjusted player on their side, a kicker with a slender frame that looks almost childlike among the enhanced giants.

"National anthem," Coach barks, and they line up along the sideline, hands over hearts. Hal catches Jackson wincing as he raises his arm, a lingering injury from last week that would have healed instantly with regeneration nanites, but Jackson's contract doesn't cover the expensive treatment.

The coin toss goes their way. Offense first.

In the huddle, quarterback Martinez's eyes gleam with an intimidating golden sheen. "Spider-two Y banana, on two. Hal, you're the primary look if they show blitz."

Hal nods, already visualizing the route, the defender's likely movements, the small window of opportunity that will open for precisely 0.8 seconds. His bulk enhancement isn't just about strength—it's about precision, about applying exactly the right amount of force at the right moment.

"Break!"

They explode from the huddle into formation. Across the line of scrimmage, the Baron's middle linebacker—a mountain of a man with dermal reinforcement nanites that make his skin look like polished granite—points directly at Hal.

"Eighty-eight! Watch eighty-eight!"

Hal smiles behind his face mask. They always watch him, and he still finds ways to make them pay.

"Hut! Hut!"

The ball snaps and time slows. This is where the bulk nanites truly shine, enhancing not just his strength but his perception. While an unadjusted player might see chaos, Hal sees patterns, trajectories, opportunities—his brain working overtime. The defensive end crashes down, leaving a gap. Hal erupts through it, muscles generating force that would tear normal human tendons from bone.

The linebacker meets him five yards downfield, a collision that sends a shock wave through the stadium. The seconds stretch on as they're locked together. The taste of grass and dirt fills Hal's mouth. It's not entirely unpleasant. The linebacker grunts. Then Hal feels the subtle shift of weight, the microsecond of imbalance. He drives his legs, pushes with calculated force, and suddenly he's free, running to freedom and glory.

Fifty yards later, the crowd is on its feet, and Hal is in the end zone, ball raised triumphantly.

First touchdown of the game. He doesn't dance or pose, just hands the ball to the official and jogs back to the sideline, accepting high-fives as he goes.

"That's what I'm talking about!" Martinez slaps his helmet. "They can't stop the freight train!"

Coach Decker just nods, as if the play was expected. "Good read, Small. Good execution."

The game flows on. Nearing halftime, the Reapers lead 21-14, with Hal responsible for two touchdowns. Hal winces as an enhanced wall of muscle tears into Jackson, sending him sprawling across the turf. But as his unadjusted teammate struggles to his feet, the fire in his eyes shows pure determination.

But it's only five minutes later when Jackson finds himself in the crosshairs of one of the Barons' enhanced linebackers. The linebacker charges at Jackson with an intensity that sends shivers through the crowd.

The moment stretches into eternity as spectators hold their breaths in anticipation. Hal holds his breath too. Then, with an impact that echoes across the stadium, they collide.

Jackson crumples as if he were made of paper rather than flesh and bone. His knee twists unnaturally under him, buckling under the force of the tackle. A sickening snap cuts through the air. A sound no one ever wants to hear on a football field.

The crowd gasps collectively as realization dawns; that was not just any noise but the gruesome rip of tendons tearing. The stadium falls silent, save for Jackson's agonized groan echoing hauntingly across the field.

Hal jogs over to him. Jackson blinks in recognition, grips Hal's outstretched hand, squeezes all his pain into it. Hal can take it. Hell, he can barely feel it.

"Just breathe," Hal tells him. "Breathe through the pain."

Jackson rasps for breath. A couple minutes later medics arrive with a stretcher. Hal lifts his teammate onto the stretcher and watches as he's carted away. He catches eyes with Miller, sees the fear in his eyes, knowing it could have been him. The football field is no longer a place for unadjusteds. But most of them can't afford the bulk nanite or are still saving up for it. He likes Jackson. And Miller and Ramierz. He doesn't want them to get hurt, and he knows they'd all refuse to step down. But they're going to get hurt if they stay.

There's only one more play until the halftime whistle sounds. Neither team scores.

"Should've bulked up." Hal overhears one of the rookie enhanced players mutter about Jackson as Hal heads to the locker room. "What's he thinking, playing natural against bulks?"

Hal frowns but says nothing. As he grabs a cup of water, he spots Jackson in the rehab room. A team of doctors with grim expressions are working on him as his mouth twists with pain. Without regeneration nanites, he's done for the game, maybe longer.

"You're killing them out there, Small." Coach finds him by the water fountain, droplets carelessly dribbling down his chin. "They've got no answer for your power game."

Hal nods, but his eyes drift to Jackson, now wearing a brace on his knee. "What's the word on Jackson?"

Coach's face tightens. "MCL sprain. He's done."

"His contract cover regen nanites?"

"That's between him and management." Coach turns away, but the answer is clear enough. Lower-tier players, especially unadjusted ones, rarely get the premium medical benefits. Hal sends up a quick prayer that he had the foresight to sign with a fantastic agent who made sure his contract took care of him. And he's going to make damn sure his new contract comes with all the bells and whistles.

The second half begins with renewed intensity. The Barons adjust their defense, double-teaming Hal on every play. It creates opportunities for others, but the physical toll mounts. Ramirez takes a brutal hit over the middle, his unadjusted body crumpling under the impact of a member of the opposition whose reflexes and strength have been enhanced to the legal limit. Or maybe beyond. More and more documents are being forged, signed off by doctors with a wad of cash sent under the table.

The crowd gasps, then falls silent as medical staff rush onto the field. Hal watches, the familiar unease coiling in his stomach. Ramirez eventually sits up, woozy but conscious, and is helped off the field.

Two unadjusted players down, one remaining.

With six minutes left in the fourth quarter and the score tied at 28, Miller, the last unadjusted Reaper still playing, fumbles after a jarring hit. The Barons recover and score, taking the lead. Miller is subbed out. He sits alone on the bench, head in his hands, while the enhanced players avoid eye contact.

"Not his fault," Hal says to Martinez, as they prepare for the final drive. "Any of us would've dropped it after a hit like that."

Martinez raises an eyebrow. "Maybe. But that's kind of the point, isn't it? We don't take hits like that."

Two-minute warning. Down by seven. Eighty yards to go.

This is where Hal earns his contract. On first down, he breaks three tackles for a twelve-yard gain. Second play, he pancakes a blitzing linebacker, giving Martinez time to find Dominguez for thirty yards. The stadium thrums with energy as they cross midfield.

"They're tired," Hal says in the huddle, tasting victory. "Front side's overplaying. Counter will be there."

Martinez nods. "Counter 38 Blast on one. Ready? Break!"

The play unfolds like a dream. The defensive line shifts exactly as Hal predicted, overcommitting to his initial movement. He takes the handoff, plants his foot, and cuts back against the grain. One defender has stayed home—their free safety, an enhanced player known for his closing speed.

Their gazes collide. They are alone in space, a one-on-one confrontation that will decide the game. The safety launches himself, a perfectly timed missile. But energy sings in Hal's veins, and he makes a cut that should be impossible for a man his size. The safety grazes him, fingers sliding off his jersey, and then there's nothing but open field.

Sixty thousand fans rise as one as Hal crosses the goal line. Tie game, thirty seconds left. The extra point gives them the lead, and the defense holds for a dramatic victory. Four more years. All of Hal's dreams are coming true. He looks up at the stands, sees his wife holding their sleeping son, and smiles. He wishes he could pause this moment and stay in it forever.

In the locker room, champagne flows. Hal accepts congratulations and banter with his teammates, but his eyes keep drifting to the training room where team doctors work on Jackson and Ramirez.

"MVP! MVP!" The chant starts with Dominguez and spreads through the locker room. Coach Decker appears with the game ball.

"No surprise here. Player of the game...Hal Small!"

The ball lands in his hands to thunderous applause. Hal

raises it briefly, acknowledging the honor. As the cameras flash and reporters press forward, he can't help thinking about the players in the training room, wondering if their contracts might suddenly include regeneration nanites if they'd made the game-winning play instead.

"How does it feel, Hal?" asks a reporter, thrusting a microphone toward him.

Hal chooses his words carefully. "Just doing my job. Team victory today."

"Are you going to let anyone else get a few seconds in the limelight?" a pretty, blonde reporter asks.

"Always happy to share," Hal replies.

"And he's far too modest for his own good," Coach cuts in. "You won that game, and I think you'll find the powers that be may have to add another zero to that contract."

Hal can't help but grin. That would set him and Mara up for life. And they could start a college fund for Brandon.

Coach drags him and a couple of other players into the press room. Hal has been in here countless times before, but he never gets used to the brightness of the lights or the sound of the cameras clicking.

He sits at the center of the long table, and smiles politely at the forest of microphones.

"Hal, that's your third straight game with over a hundred fifty yards," calls out a reporter from the front row, her eyes glowing with inhuman light. "Does it feel like you're reaching a new level this season?"

"Offensive line is creating great opportunities. Martinez is making the right reads. It's a team effort," Hal replies.

"But you're the one making the impossible plays," another

reporter chimes in. "That cut on the final touchdown... physics says a man your size shouldn't be able to change direction that quickly."

Hal shifts slightly. "That's what the nanites are for, I guess."

"Speaking of which," an older reporter leans forward, "three unadjusted players were injured today. Do you think there's still a place for naturals in the modern game?"

The question hangs in the air. Hal feels a flicker of annoyance at the term "naturals," the subtle implication that enhanced players are somehow unnatural.

"Jackson, Ramirez, and Miller are elite athletes who've earned their spots on this team. The game's evolving, sure, but football has always been about more than physical attributes. It's about heart, intelligence, work ethic."

"But realistically," the reporter presses, "given the speed and strength of enhanced players, isn't it irresponsible to field unadjusted players? For their own safety?"

"I think everyone deserves the right to choose," Hal says, his voice firmer now. "Some players have religious objections to nanites. Some have medical contradictions. Some just want to play the game as they are. That's their decision."

Coach Decker leans in. "Two more questions, folks. We've got a reception to get to."

After fielding softballs about next week's matchup, Hal escapes the press room, nodding appreciatively at the staff who hold doors for him. The stadium corridors are quieter now, most fans departed, but team personnel and security still bustle about. Outside the locker room, he pauses when he hears raised voices.

"—league minimum for what? To watch him get carted off every other game?" It's Thornton, one of the defensive tackles, his voice carrying through the half-open door. "Management needs to stop wasting roster spots on unadjusteds."

Hal's jaw tightens at the edge in Thornton's tone.

"Miller's got a wife and kid," someone else replies. "Not everyone won the nanite lottery like you did at USC."

"Not my problem," Thornton says. "Football's an enhanced sport now. Unadjusteds should stick to, I don't know, badminton or whatever."

Hal pushes the door open. The conversation stops abruptly as he enters. Thornton has the decency to look embarrassed, but doesn't back down.

"Just saying what everyone's thinking, Small."

"Not what I'm thinking," Hal replies, keeping his voice level despite the anger simmering beneath. "Those unadjusteds you're talking about? They're our teammates. They bleed for this team same as you."

"Yeah, difference is they bleed a lot more," another player chimes in, earning scattered laughter.

Hal opens his locker, shoulders tight. "Easy to talk big when you've got class-nine durability nanites, isn't it? Some guys make a choice not to enhance. Others can't afford it. Either way, they deserve respect."

"It's not about respect," Thornton argues. "It's about reality. The game's faster, harder than it was twenty years ago. Unadjusteds can't keep up without getting wrecked. That's just facts."

"I wouldn't be here without my bulk enhancement," Hal

admits, fishing his street clothes from his locker. "But I got lucky. Junior year of high school, community raffle for one class-ten nanite. One in ten thousand odds, and I hit it. Without that? Who knows."

The locker room quiets, players listening now. Hal rarely talks about how he got his enhancement.

"Before that, I was just another kid from the east side with decent hands and average speed," he continues, pulling on his shirt. "My parents couldn't have afforded a basic class-three, let alone a bulk. So when I see guys like Miller playing unadjusted? That's not weakness. That's courage."

Thornton looks away, not quite convinced but unwilling to argue further. "Whatever, man. Just hate seeing guys carted off when a simple pill could prevent it."

The conversation shifts to safer topics as Hal finishes changing. He checks his phone. There's a message from Mara asking if he'll be late. He texts back that he has to make an appearance at the VIP reception but will be home soon after. As he pockets his phone, he notices Jackson hobbling in, knee heavily braced.

"Hey," Hal says, moving to help him to his locker. "How bad?"

"Grade two MCL sprain," Jackson replies, grimacing as he sits. "Eight weeks, minimum."

"Your contract cover regen nanites?"

Jackson laughs without humor. "What do you think? I'm a fifth-round pick on a rookie deal. I'm lucky they're paying for the MRI."

Hal nods, understanding all too well. "Season's not over. You'll be back."

"Maybe," Jackson says, but they both know the truth, eight weeks on the sideline means his roster spot might not be waiting for him when he returns.

They shake hands and Hal pulls him in for a one-armed hug before he leaves for the swanky reception.

The VIP lounge glitters with wealth, the air perfumed with expensive colognes and enhanced pheromones. Sponsors and season ticket holders mingle with players, the social hierarchy as visible as the quality of their clothing. Hal navigates the space, accepting congratulations, signing the occasional autograph, posing for photos with wide-smiling executives.

"There he is!" A portly man with artificially whitened teeth waves Hal over. "The man of the hour!"

Hal recognizes him as Ellison, a major team sponsor whose security company provides facial recognition systems to several stadiums. Beside him stands another executive, thin and severe looking.

"Incredible performance today, Small," Ellison says, pumping Hal's hand. "Simply incredible."

"Thank you, sir. I appreciate that. It's always nice to hear good things."

"Nice?" Ellison laughs. "Jersey sales up thirty percent this quarter! That's better than *nice*."

The thin executive eyes Hal with professional assessment. "The bulk enhancement is Nanocorp's model B1.0, correct? How long have you had it?"

"Since high school," Hal replies. "Over ten years now."

"Remarkable longevity," the man nods approvingly. "Most

first-generation bulks show degradation after a decade. You must have exceptional genetic compatibility."

Hal shrugs, heat pooling on the back of his neck. "Guess I'm lucky."

"More than lucky," Ellison says. "Smart! Not like these young idiots still trying to play unadjusted. Did you see that fumble today? Shameful."

Something cold settles in Hal's stomach. "Miller took a hit that would've broken an enhanced player's ribs. The fact he held onto the ball as long as he did was impressive."

Ellison waves dismissively. "If he can't afford enhancement, he shouldn't be in the league. It's irresponsible."

"Not everyone wants enhancement," Hal says quietly.

They both look at him blankly, reassessing. The cool of the air conditioning funnels down Hal's shirt, but it does nothing to thaw the heat on his cheeks.

"Then they need to get out of the game," Ellison says.

The thin man nods. "The league is evolving. Unadjusted players are becoming a liability. Insurance rates, injury time-outs disrupting game flow, negative fan perception when stars are sidelined."

"When I was coming up, I couldn't have afforded enhancement," Hal says. "If I hadn't won that raffle, I'd have been just another kid with potential who never got the chance. Is that the future we want? Where only the wealthy get enhancements and opportunities?"

An uncomfortable silence falls. Ellison's smile becomes fixed.

"Well," he says finally, "I should mingle. Wonderful game today, Small. Truly wonderful."

Hal curses as they walk away. He's media trained. He knows how to nod along like one of the dashboard toys. But why didn't he? Because he's sick of the injustice, of the growing divide, of the way people might treat his unadjusted wife. She's never complained, never mentioned prejudice, but now Hal wonders.

A hand claps his shoulder, and he turns to find Pearson, the team's general manager, standing behind him.

"Easy on the social justice, Small," Pearson says, his tone light but his eyes serious. "Ellison's company is up for contract renewal next season."

"Sorry," Hal says, not feeling particularly sorry. "Just tired of the attitude."

Pearson guides him to a quieter corner. "Look, I get it. But you need to understand the direction the league is heading. Fans want spectacle. Sponsors want reliability. Both mean more enhancements, not fewer."

"And players who choose to remain unadjusted, or can't afford enhancement?"

"The market decides," Pearson says with the finality of someone stating an immutable law. "Just like it always has."

Later, as Hal waits for his car at the VIP exit, he watches a group of fans gathered behind the security barrier. Children wave jerseys and footballs, hoping for autographs. One boy, no more than ten, wears Hal's number 88. Beside him, a slightly older girl holds a sign: "MILLER #17 - UNADJUSTED HERO."

Hal walks over, signs their items, poses for photos. The girl with the Miller sign beams at him.

"My dad says Miller's the bravest player because he

doesn't use nanites," she tells Hal. "He says that's real football."

Hal smiles, but inside, his unease grows. He wonders how long *real football* will exist for players like Miller, Jackson, and Ramirez. How long before the economics that Pearson speaks of with such certainty reshape the game completely? And what responsibility does he, with his lucky bulk enhancement, have to those left behind?

CHAPTER 2

THE PROJECTOR's light cuts through the darkness of the meeting room like a surgeon's laser, illuminating the faces of twenty-three professional football players.

Hal shifts in his seat, the plastic chair creaking under his weight. The Baltimore game replays in high definition, every mistake, every missed block, every fumbled opportunity magnified on the wall. Coach Decker stands at the front, remote in hand, his jaw set in that particular way that means someone's about to get chewed out. Hal can already feel the divide in the room—altered players on one side, the two unadjusteds on the other. He sits in the middle, some kind of bridge that he doesn't think will last much longer.

"This right here." Coach Decker freezes the frame, jabbing his finger at the screen where Miller gets flattened by a Baltimore bulk. "This is what I'm talking about. Miller, you're giving him the inside lane every single time. You know bulks have increased speed, strength and reflexes. You've got to anticipate, not react."

Miller nods tightly. "Yes, Coach."

"And here—" Coach clicks forward to another play. "Jackson misses his assignment completely because he's busy helping Ramirez who got pancaked by their defensive end."

The tension in the room thickens. The altered players exchange knowing glances. The two unadjusteds stare straight ahead, jaws clenched, taking the criticism on the chin because they have no choice.

"Look, I'm not pointing fingers," Coach Decker continues. "I'm identifying problems so we can solve them. As a team."

That last word rings hollow, but no one calls him out. Not even Hal. He values his career. And his life.

"With all due respect, Coach," Dominguez speaks up from the back row, "some problems can't be solved with practice and film study."

Coach Decker raises an eyebrow. "What are you suggesting, Dominguez?"

"I'm suggesting maybe some guys need to consider their options." Dominguez's eyes sweep across the unadjusted players. "The league is evolving. Either evolve with it or get left behind."

The temperature in the room drops ten degrees.

"That's out of line," Ramirez, an unadjusted veteran, says quietly. "We're all here because we earned our spots."

"Did you, though?" This from Tanner, the largest bulk in the team. "Or are you here to prove some kind of unadjusted point?"

Coach Decker raises his hands. "Let's stay focused on the game, gentlemen."

"That is the game now, Coach," Dominguez insists. "Look

at L.A. One hundred percent altered, and they're undefeated. Cincinnati, same thing. Meanwhile, we're getting our asses handed to us because three of our players think taking a nanite is somehow cheating."

"We did *not* get our asses handed to us." Ramirez stands up, his chair screeching against the floor. "And some of us don't want to swallow a pill that rewrites who we are as human beings. Some of us still believe that football is about heart and skill, not who has the most expensive modifications."

"Heart and skill?" Tanner snorts. "Tell that to the scoreboard. Tell that to the fans who want championships."

"We won, didn't we?" Hal cuts in.

"Just." Tanner pins his eyes on Hal. "What about the next game, and the one after that?"

Dominguez smirks. "Jackson and Ramirez are both injured, so the next game won't be a problem."

"Enough." Coach Decker's voice cracks like a whip. But Hal notices something that makes his stomach twist—the coach isn't looking at Tanner or Dominguez. His stern gaze is fixed on Ramirez and Miller. "Sentimentality doesn't win games. Performance does. And right now, our performance isn't cutting it."

A charged silence follows. The unspoken meaning hangs in the air.

The guilt hits Hal like a linebacker to the gut. He remembers what it was like to play on an uneven field. Remembers the sprains and bruised ribs. Remembers the desperation of giving up the game he loves because he couldn't afford a nanite. And then the raffle changed everything. And if he was still unadjusted? Mara would never let him play. He has a son to live for.

"Coach," Hal says, unable to quieten his inner voice. "Maybe we're approaching this wrong. The mistakes we made during the Baltimore game happened because we played as individuals instead of a team."

Coach Decker fixes him with a stare that could strip paint. "Interesting perspective from someone who clearly benefited from enhancement."

The words sting, but Hal pushes through. "My enhancement doesn't make me a better teammate. It doesn't make me see the field better or understand our playbook. The fully enhanced teams might be stronger, but they're predictable. Their plays are always the same, always about brute strength—"

"Yeah," Domingues laughs. "That's kind of the point."

Hal ignores him. "Jackson and Ramierz got injured because we're divided, not because of who has or hasn't taken a nanite."

"Easy for you to say," Miller mutters. "You're a bulk. Have been since the beginning of your career."

"I'm just saying..." Hal trails off.

"When was the last time you sat with the unadjusteds in the cafeteria?" Miller asks. "When was the last time you didn't use your enhancement to show off in practice?"

"I don't show off," Hal protests, heat rising to his face.

"You don't have to," Ramirez says. "Your very existence is showing off. Walking proof that enhancement is the only way forward."

Coach Decker clears his throat. "Hal does have a point

about teamwork, but the reality is that the league is changing. President Bear's policies are clear. Evolution is the future. And frankly, I've got a responsibility to put the best team on the field."

"Even if that means pushing out players who choose to remain unadjusted?" Miller asks.

"My hands are tied," Coach responds. "There are sponsors to appease."

Hal stands up, unable to contain the energy bubbling through his limbs. "Listen, we can make this work. The unadjusteds bring intelligence and experience that the nanites can't replicate. The altered players bring physical advantages. Together, we're better than those other teams."

"Sooner or later, Small, you're going to have to pick a side," Thornton says, folding his arms across his chest. "The days of straddling the fence are coming to an end."

"I'm not picking sides," Hal insists. "I'm on this team's side."

"There's no middle ground anymore," Tanner says, standing up to his full height, his enhanced frame casting a shadow over Hal. "You're either with progress or against it. You're either altered or you're obsolete."

"Fuck you." Ramirez lurches out of his chair and leaves, slamming the door behind him.

Miller pushes to his feet, the only unadjusted left in the room, locks gazes with a few teammates, then turns on his heel and follows Ramirez.

Coach Decker ends the meeting with a curt reminder about tomorrow's practice schedule, but the damage is done. As the players file out, his altered teammates eye Hal with suspicion, as if his defense of the unadjusteds has marked him as a traitor.

Hal is the last one to leave the room. In the silence, he imagines he can hear the faint whirring of the nanites in his bloodstream, recalibrating his muscles, optimizing his cellular structure. Making him better. Making him different.

Making him choose.

)0(0(0(0(

The Helix Lounge sits like a gleaming spaceship among Central City's downtown high-rises, all curved glass and pulsing lights that change color with the collective mood of its patrons.

Hal guides Mara through the revolving door, his hand at the small of her back. Inside, the restaurant hums with energy. They've been on the waiting list for months, and after last week's win, Hal got a phone call saying they were in. But as he casts his eyes around the swanky restaurant, he wonders if it is good idea. He can't spot a single individual besides Mara who looks unadjusted.

He takes in the soft fluttering of decorative wings, the metallic gleam of reinforced skin catching the light, horns arguing with dangling chandeliers, color-changing skin that compliments the surroundings. The plethora of enhancements is mindboggling. When did they invent all of these?

Watching the hostess' eyes flicker over Mara's conspicuously unenhanced features, Hal wishes he'd suggested somewhere else entirely.

"Reservation for Small," Hal says, squaring his shoulders.

The hostess, her skin embedded with what must be thousands of tiny LED lights that pulse in patterns beneath her translucent blouse, smiles at Hal with immediate recognition. "Mr. Small, of course. The Central City Reapers' star." Her gaze slides to Mara with noticeably less warmth. "And guest."

"My wife," Hal corrects. "Mara Small."

"Of course." The hostess' eyes narrow. "Follow me, please."

They weave through tables where the city's elite display their enhancements like peacocks fanning their feathers. A woman with emerald-scaled skin throws her head back in laughter, the sound amplified by a vocal modification that makes it ring like crystal. Two business executives with subtle cranial bulges lock eyes across their table in silent neurotransmission, their conversation happening on a plane Hal and Mara can't access.

Mara squeezes Hal's hand. "Quite the scene," she whispers.

Although Hal can tell she is nervous, she has never looked more beautiful. An electric blue figure-hugging dress that sets off her eyes.

The hostess leads them not to the center of the restaurant where most patrons are seated, but to a small table tucked away near the kitchen entrance. "Will this be suitable?" she asks, though it's clearly not a question.

Hal glances at the main dining area where other patrons chat beneath a ceiling that shifts and swirls with projected images of DNA strands morphing into artistic patterns. Their table sits beneath a static section of ceiling, the lighting noticeably dimmer.

"Actually," Hal begins, but Mara cuts him off with a gentle touch to his arm.

"This is fine," she says. "Thank you."

The hostess leaves them with digital menus that activate with a touch, the screens illuminating with options. Hal watches Mara's face as she scrolls through dishes designed to showcase the chef's molecular gastronomy enhancements.

"I'm sorry about this," Hal says quietly. "I made this reservation before..."

She smiles. "Before what?"

Hal blows out a breath. "I'm not sure, really, but this is not what I was expecting."

Mara leans over the table, playing with the fake candle flame. "What were you expecting?"

Hal lifts a shoulder. "Something...fun? Expensive? Exquisite food? A restaurant befitting a queen...you."

Mara laughs. "It is all of those things."

"Maybe."

She touches his arm, a too-light touch on his armored skin. A definite downside to the enhancement. "I want to try the famous hovering soufflé everyone's been talking about."

Their waiter appears beside them. His enhancement is immediately obvious. Colorful tattoos swirl over his skin, blooming on his neck to disappear beneath his head. And he smells like a pine forest mixed with musky, masculine spice. He must have opted for ScentSkin.

"Good evening, Mr. Small," the waiter says, his voice honeyed with admiration. "It's an honor to serve you tonight. I'm Jules. The chef has prepared several specials for altered patrons this evening." His gaze flickers to Mara, his expression cooling. "We also have some traditional options."

The way he says "traditional"—like it's a synonym for "primitive"—makes Hal's jaw clench.

"What would you recommend for my wife?" Hal asks pointedly.

Jules blinks, as if surprised by the question. "Perhaps the poached salmon? It's... straightforward. Easily digestible for unmodified systems."

Mara's smile tightens. "Actually, I'd like to try the neural-nebula pasta. The one that changes flavor based on the diner's mood."

Jules shifts uncomfortably. "That dish is designed to interact with the enhanced sensory receptors most of our clientele possess. Without the proper nanite adjustments, it would just taste like...well, plain pasta."

"I'll take my chances," Mara says, her voice gentle but firm.

Jules looks to Hal as if for permission or perhaps rescue from this awkward exchange.

"You heard my wife," Hal says. "And I'll have the same."

"Very well." Jules' tattoos flicker. "And to drink? We have several beverages that react to altered body chemistry, creating unique flavor profiles for each guest."

"Just water for me," Mara says.

"A bottle of the Cabernet," Hal counters. "The regular kind. No enhancements necessary."

As Jules drifts away, Hal reaches across the table to take Mara's hand. "I should have realized this place would be like this."

"Like what?" Mara asks, though they both know exactly what he means.

"Engineered for people who've taken the leap into modification. Unwelcoming to everyone else."

Mara shrugs. "It's becoming the norm, Hal. You know that. Brandon's preschool teacher suggested we consider a basic enhancement package for him. Said it would 'help him keep up with his peers.'" She shakes her head. "He's two years old."

"I thought they were unsafe for kids under twelve?"

Mara raises both brows. "They are. But it doesn't stop some parents."

The anger that's been simmering in Hal since the team meeting threatens to boil over. Before he can respond, Jules returns with their wine and two glasses. He pours a taste for Hal with practiced precision, ignoring Mara completely.

"Excellent choice, sir," Jules says after Hal takes a perfunctory sip.

Two tables over, a woman with butterfly wings similar to those Hal sees on the cheerleading squad whispers something to her companion, eyes darting to Mara. They both laugh behind manicured hands.

Other patrons' eyes linger on Mara with curiosity or disdain, then flick to him with something like betrayal. An altered man and professional athlete should not be dining with an unmodified woman, their stares seem to say.

When their appetizers arrive, CRISPR Croquetts (golden fried bites containing mood-enhancing adaptogens and color-coded filling) for Hal, a simple plate for Mara despite ordering the same dish, Hal's patience begins to fray.

"Excuse me," he says as Jules starts to leave. "My wife ordered the same appetizer I did."

Jules' tattoos turn midnight black. "The chef felt the unmodified version would be more appropriate for Madam."

"That wasn't his decision to make," Hal says, a dangerous edge creeping into his tone.

"It's fine, Hal," Mara murmurs. "Really."

But it isn't fine. None of this is fine.

As they eat, the staff's behavior grows increasingly blatant. Water glasses are refilled for altered patrons while Mara's remains empty. Complimentary between-course palate cleansers come to every table except theirs. The way the sommelier approaches to check on their wine but addresses only Hal, as if Mara is invisible.

When Jules brings their main courses, Hal overhears him mutter to another server by the kitchen door, "Table twelve. Unmodified wife. Probably can't even taste the difference between this and fast food."

The other server, a woman with gills pulsing subtly at her neck, laughs. "Why do they even come here? There are plenty of restaurants for unadjusteds in the east district."

Hal's fork clatters against his plate. Mara looks up, startled.

"What's wrong?"

"Nothing," Hal says, but his muscles are coiled tight.

The meal continues with growing tension. The neural-nebula pasta on Mara's plate remains stubbornly uninspired. The chef has clearly provided her with an inferior version of the dish. Hal's own meal shifts and changes with his emotions, currently turning a dark, angry red that tastes of smoke and metal.

When Jules approaches again to check on their meal, Hal has had enough.

"Is there a problem?" Hal asks, his voice controlled but carrying an edge that makes nearby conversations falter.

Jules raises a heavily pierced eyebrow. "Not at all, sir. Is something unsatisfactory?"

"You tell me," Hal says. "You've refilled my water three times and ignored my wife's empty glass. You brought her a different appetizer than what she ordered. And I heard your comment by the kitchen door."

The waiter's tattoos flicker rapidly. "I—I apologize if there's been a misunderstanding—"

"There's no misunderstanding," Hal cuts him off. "You and the rest of the staff have treated my wife with disrespect from the moment we walked in. Is this how The Helix Lounge treats all unadjusted customers, or just the ones who have the audacity to dine with their altered spouses?"

The restaurant has grown quieter, attention turning to their table. Jules' tattoos stabilize as he straightens his spine. "Sir, perhaps you're being oversensitive. We pride ourselves on exceptional service for all our guests."

"*All* your guests?" Hal stands, his bulk form towering over the waiter. "Or just the ones you deem worthy because they've modified their bodies?"

"Hal," Mara says softly, "please sit down."

But Hal can't back down now. The same feeling that drove him to defend his unadjusted teammates pulses through him. "I'd like to speak to the manager."

Jules nods stiffly and disappears toward the back of the restaurant. Several long, uncomfortable minutes pass. Mara sips her wine, her composure unwavering even as curious and judgmental eyes turn their way.

The manager who approaches their table has the unmistakable bearing of someone with multiple cosmetic enhancements. He has perfectly symmetrical features and subtle gold flecks in his irises.

"Mr. Small," he says, his voice modulated to project authority and calm simultaneously. "I understand there's been some dissatisfaction with your experience this evening. Please accept my apologies for any perceived slight."

The word "perceived" makes Hal's blood boil. "There was nothing perceived about it. Your staff have treated my wife like a second-class citizen all evening."

The manager glances at Mara, his expression a mask of professional concern. "That would certainly be unacceptable if true. Perhaps there has been a miscommunication. The Helix Lounge prides itself on creating an environment where the enhanced community can fully express and experience their modifications." He pauses delicately. "We do welcome all guests, of course, but our establishment is specifically designed to cater to the unique needs and capabilities of altered patrons."

"Meaning what, exactly?" Hal asks.

The manager's smile is practiced, perfect. "Meaning, perhaps, there might be other establishments better suited to...mixed couples such as yourselves. Places where everyone can feel comfortable."

Hal pushes back his chair. "You mean segregated restaurants. Places where unadjusteds know their place."

"That's not what I—"

"It's exactly what you meant," Hal says. He pulls out his wallet and places several large bills on the table. "This should cover our barely-touched meals and your staff's bigotry."

He turns to Mara, who is already gathering her purse, her face a carefully composed mask that breaks Hal's heart. Has she been treated like this before? Has she dealt with it quietly? Has she decided not to confide in him?

"Let's go," he says more gently.

As they walk toward the exit, conversations resume around them, some patrons shooting disapproving glances, others looking uncomfortable or even ashamed. A few nod slightly to Hal, a silent acknowledgment that perhaps he wasn't entirely wrong.

The hostess with the LED skin avoids eye contact as they pass. Outside, the cool night air feels cleansing after the stifling atmosphere of enforced evolution inside. Mara takes Hal's hand, her touch grounding him, bringing him back from the edge of his anger.

"I'm sorry about that," Hal says as they walk toward their car. "I shouldn't have made a scene."

Mara squeezes his hand. "Actually, I'm glad you did." Her voice carries an unexpected note of pride. "Most enhanced people just...look through me these days. Like I'm a relic of the past. It's nice to know you still see me."

The simple statement hits Hal like a tackle, knocking the wind from his lungs. Has he been truly seeing her? Or has he been so caught up in his own struggles with his athletic reputation that he's missed what she's been going through?

"Always," he promises.

He takes Mara's hand and guides her to the car, opens the door for her, even buckles her in. He will never, ever, not even for a second, take his wife for granted again. Whether she remains unadjusted or chooses to become enhanced, he will support her in every decision. And she will be loved. He will show her that love, every single goddamn day.

He makes these promises to himself on the drive home, glances at her profile as often as it's safe while he's driving, can't wait to take her into his arms.

When they park in their drive, the porch light casts a welcoming glow over their two-story home. Hal again opens the door for Mara, and she giggles and delights in his new acts of chivalry.

"Who said football players can't be romantic?" she teases as they walk through the front door.

Inside, the babysitter looks up from her textbook. Her unadjusted features cause a slice of pain to stab through Hal. Her future will be difficult. If she remains unadjusted.

She smiles at them, tucking a strand of natural blonde hair behind her ear. No LED skin. No modified vocal cords. No wings or horns or animated tattoos. Just a normal nineteen-year-old trying to make tuition money in a world that's increasingly leaving her kind behind.

"How was he?" Mara asks, shrugging off her jacket.

"Perfect," Jenny says, closing her biology textbook. "We read three stories, built a tower that reached the ceiling, and he only asked for you guys twice before falling asleep."

Hal notices the title of Jenny's textbook: "Evolutionary Biology in the Nanite Age." Her highlighting pens and notes are meticulously organized, the work of someone who knows she can't rely on intelligence enhancements to compete with her classmates.

"Did you get much studying done?" he asks, reaching for his wallet.

Jenny nods. "I have a big exam tomorrow. Professor Collins gives different tests to enhanced and unenhanced students. Says it's 'equitable assessment' but the unadjusted track is killing me."

Hal pulls out extra cash and adds a generous tip. "You're smart. You'll do great."

"Thanks for the vote of confidence," Jenny says, as she gathers her things. "Same time next week?"

"That would be perfect," Mara confirms, walking her to the door.

As Jenny leaves, Hal catches a glimpse of her scholarship application peeking from her backpack. The university's logo prominently displays their new slogan: "Evolving Excellence." The irony isn't lost on him.

"Let's check on Brandon," Mara whispers, already heading up the stairs.

Their son's room is awash in the soft blue light of his constellation projector, stars dancing across the ceiling in scientifically accurate patterns. It was a gift from Hal's parents who believe in educational toys. Brandon lies sprawled on his back, one arm flung dramatically over his head, the other clutching his favorite stuffed dinosaur. His chest rises and falls with the deep, untroubled breathing of childhood.

Hal feels the familiar tug in his heart as he looks at his son. Brandon's curly brown hair falls across his forehead in a way that reminds Hal of his own childhood photos. His round cheeks still carry the softness of toddlerhood, flushed pink with sleep. Completely natural. Untouched by the nanite revolution.

Mara adjusts the blanket that Brandon has kicked to the foot of his bed, tucking it gently around him.

"Do you ever think about it?" Hal whispers. "What he'll face when he's older?"

Mara's hand finds his in the darkness. "Every day."

They close the door softly behind them and head down-stairs. The living room welcomes them with familiar comfort —a worn leather couch, family photos documenting their history together, Brandon's toys overflowing from colorful bins. Mara retrieves a bottle of wine from the rack while Hal plumps the cushions.

"Glass?" Mara offers, already pouring.

Hal accepts, settling onto the couch.

"Hell of a night," he says after a long sip.

Mara kicks off her shoes and curls her legs beneath her on the couch. "The pasta wasn't even that good. Regular or enhanced version."

Her attempt at lightness falls flat. The evening's ugly reality sits between them like an unwelcome guest.

"That wasn't an isolated incident," Hal says finally. "What happened at the restaurant. It's happening everywhere. The team is fracturing. Coach Decker practically told the unadjusted players they're holding us back."

"Hmm," Mara murmurs noncommittally, swirling her wine.

"And the looks people gave us tonight," Hal continues, the frustration building again. "Like you didn't belong there. Like we were breaking some unwritten rule by being together. A month ago, I wouldn't have noticed, but now..." He shakes his head. "It's like there are two different worlds emerging, and the gap between them is getting wider every day."

Mara runs a finger along the arm of the couch. "You're just noticing it now because you're straddling both sides. For the rest of us, this has been reality for a while."

Her calm acceptance catches Hal off guard. "What do you mean?"

"I mean," Mara says, setting down her glass, "that while you've been playing football and hanging out with your bulk teammates, I've been living in a world that's increasingly hostile to people who choose to remain unadjusted. The grocery store has separate checkout lines now, did you notice? Fast track for speedsters. My boss hired a new assistant with organizational nanites who's already been promoted over me despite having half my experience."

Shock thrums through Hal's body. He might be a bulk with armored skin, but his emotions are as raw as ever. "Why haven't you said anything?"

Mara shrugs. "What would be the point? It's just how things are now. President Bear's policies are clear. Evolution is the path forward. The Nanite Representation Agency has already set out a suggested pathway for children from the age of twelve."

"And that doesn't worry you?" Hal leans forward, searching her face.

"Of course it does," Mara says, toying with a loose thread on one of the cushions. "But worrying doesn't change reality. We adapt to what is, not what we wish would be."

"By 'adapt,' do you mean take nanites?" Hal asks.

Mara meets his gaze directly. "I didn't say that. I've made my choice to remain unadjusted. At least for now. But I don't begrudge others for making different choices. Including you."

The statement hangs between them. Hal remembers the uncertainty he felt before taking the nanite. The fear that it might change who he was fundamentally. And Mara had never known him as an unadjusted. Never treated him as anything other than the man she married.

"I'm concerned about where this is all heading," Hal says. "Today it's separate checkout lines and restaurant seating. Tomorrow it could be separate neighborhoods, schools, hospitals."

"It already is, in some places," Mara says. "The east district is becoming exclusively unadjusted because property values are dropping as enhanced people move out. They've been building those new developments to accommodate wings and bulks and horns and stuff."

Hal drains his glass, the wine doing little to dull the edge of his concern. "And you're really okay with just...accepting this?"

"What's the alternative?" Mara asks. "Fight against the inevitable? The world is changing, Hal. We can rage against it, or we can find our place within it."

"Even if that place becomes smaller and more marginalized every day?"

Mara reaches for his hand. Her fingers feel delicate against his enhanced skin. "We have each other. We have Brandon. Whatever happens out there, in here we're still us."

Hal wants to believe her, but the day's events replay in his mind—the disdain in the waiter's eyes, the quiet resignation on the faces of his unadjusted teammates, Jenny's meticulous study notes for a game increasingly rigged against her. The divide isn't just happening out there. It's here, in this room, in the subtle differences between his enhanced body and Mara's unadjusted one. In the choices they'll eventually have to make for Brandon.

"I'm not sure that's enough anymore," he says.

Mara moves closer, resting her head against his shoulder. "It has to be. For now."

They sit in silence, watching the images on the TV screen rotate through Brandon's key moments. Natural. Normal. Life. Love.

Hal holds Mara closer, his enhanced strength carefully restrained, always conscious now of the power difference between them.

"I love you," he whispers into her hair.

"I know," she replies. "That's one thing that doesn't need enhancement."

Hal laughs, surprised he can feel amusement at a

moment like this. But then that is Mara, always lifting him up.

Brandon's monitor crackles and Hal is slammed into the future. Love will not reconcile the growing difference between the enhanced and the unadjusteds. Something is brewing, and it isn't going to be pretty.

CHAPTER 3

THE GLOW from Hal's laptop screen deepens the shadows in the room. Brandon's soft breathing filters through the baby monitor. Mara went to bed hours ago, a little tipsy from the second bottle of wine and exhausted from their conversation.

Hal scrubs a hand through his hair, scanning post after post from an incognito window that he hopes will hide his tracks. He'll delete the search history too. Feeling like he's doing something illegal, he can't help looking over his shoulder every five minutes at the dark hallway behind him. But so far, he can't find what he's looking for. As if an underground unadjusted movement would be stupid enough to signpost their meetings.

Hal rubs his face, his eyes begging for bed, but then he notices three emojis in the title of the next link. A DNA helix. A stop sign. And a High-five hand. He's seen them before. More than once.

And then he notices that what he thought were unintentional capital letters, actually spell out THE UNADJUSTEDS WILL SURVIVE.

Curious, he clicks on the link. Checks over his shoulder once more. Wonders if the smoke sensors are bugged somehow. Tries to dismiss the paranoia. He's a high-profile athlete, who's going to spy on him?

Hal has to answer a few questions, then he is given a password to an encrypted site. After reaffirming his identity on both his phone and his tablet, he's finally in.

He scans through the site, skimming past threads and comments complaining about discriminatory seating arrangements, restaurant staff rudeness, meals with zero flavor. He takes a deep breath. This is the first time he's heard anything about a resistance. Maybe other unadjusteds are as fed up as Mara.

The website contains more than he expected to find tonight. Hordes of people report the same treatment. And far, far worse.

A resistance is forming. *Unadjusteds, united!* The phrase repeats every few comments, a rallying cry, a manifesto. He can't wait to tell Mara about this.

He clicks to the next page, hoping to find something more substantial. Names. Something real to latch on to. One story jumps out at him: *had a reservation for three months but left before we could even order!* The comment echoes his own experience at Helix. Unmodified wife and children. Who cares about star status when we can barely afford to eat? They haven't got his fat sports contract keeping them afloat, Hal realizes. They're losing money. A follow-up comment outlines the growing pressure to take nanites, the way it builds up at school and work and in movie theatres, until it's easier to give in.

My husband lost his job because of the upgrade he refused.

They refused my daughter a college place.

My son was stabbed for refusing to take a nanite.

The situation is worse than Hal imagined. At least he still has work. At least he can afford a place to live. For now.

He shakes his head. That's the part that gets him. *For now.* How long before Bear's goons catch up with them? How long before Mara's the only unadjusted left on the whole damn planet?

He knows they can't hold out forever, but this resistance...it's something. It gives the world hope.

At the bottom of the thread, a list of meeting locations grabs his attention. He spots one nearby: *Next meeting, May 5th, 10 pm, Docks. Bring friendlies. Code word: Time to water the roots.*

They're practically begging him to show up.

Hal scrolls back up to the top of the page. He skims through more posts, soaking up the resentment, the resistance. It feels good to know he's not alone. This is real. This is something he can do. He looks back at the meeting time, committing it to memory. He'll go, scope it out, see if it's safe, then bring Mara to the next one.

✕✕✕✕✕

Hal ducks beneath a broken window and winces at the sound of his shoes echoing on the wet cement. He turns a corner to find the designated deserted warehouse and tiptoes up to the door. After placing his ear on the cold corrugated metal, he hears voices inside. Stealing himself, he pushes the door open.

He notes several bodies sitting on empty crates, several more gathered in loose circles behind them. They all look his way.

Hal raises his palm. "Time to water the roots."

The gathered people visibly exhale.

A teenaged kid with bright blue, intelligent eyes stands and comes his way. "We don't have any bulks here."

Hal scans the group. Spots one or two with wings. Another handful with enhancements that look painful or awkward, like the elderly lady with a turtle shell on her back. But the rest of them are unadjusted. Of course they are, it's their resistance after all. What the hell does Hal think he's doing here? Representing Mara and Brandon, that's what.

"Is that a problem?" Hal asks. "I've got an unadjusted wife and kid. And I sure as hell don't like the way my unadjusted teammates are being treated."

Matt gives him a once over. "You're Hal Small."

Hal nods. "Busted."

Matt smiles, genuine warmth filling his face. He offers a hand. "Welcome to the resistance. We could use a person like you."

A bulk, Hal thinks. *They need a bulk.* If the resistance gets serious, they're going have to go up against President Bear's bulk army. Unadjusteds can't do that. They need power, strength, armored skin. Hal can offer them all those things. If it means making a better future for his family, he'll sign on the dotted line.

Matt leads him closer to the group and gives a few introductions. Apparently, Matt is in charge, along with a Latino woman called Francesca and a German karate master called Claus. Interesting combo.

"You're a bulk," a teenager similar in age to Matt says. Kyle, was that his name? "You're Hal Small."

"Did you want me to sign an autograph?" Hal tests out a joke, and pleasingly, most of the gathering let out a relieved chuckle.

"You can sign my boob!" someone shouts from the back, earning another hearty round of laughter. Surprisingly, that's not the first time Hal's been asked to sign a body part.

"What's your story?" Francesa asks him.

"I didn't realize it was this bad," he says. "Not until...well, not until recently. Went out to dinner recently with my unadjusted wife and she was treated like shit."

"Helix?" Claus asks, the smallest hint of a smile.

Hal nods. "They practically shoved us out the door."

Hal scans the room one more, taking in all the serious faces, the haunted eyes, the determined jaws. "Is there a plan?"

"Absolutely," Francesca says, her voice nothing but fire.

Matt nods, adding his piece. "We're moving underground. Building networks. Scoping out safe houses. If you're part of this, you're part of it all the way."

"I'm ready," he says, "Whatever you need."

Francesca smiles, the first real smile he's seen from her. "What we need is time," she says. "This is a risk for everyone. Come back in a week. We need to vet you."

Hal stands there, caught between fear and excitement.

They're sending him away, but it means they're thinking about him. He gets it. It's more than he expected. He nods and heads for the door. Before it shuts behind him, he hears Matt's voice. "Think he'll come back?" Hal slows his pace just enough to hear Claus' reply. "We'll see."

He lingers by the door to see if he can catch a few more snatches of the conversation.

"The government has pushed us to breaking point." Francesca's voice is controlled, authoritative. "Their enhancements, their technology, it's suffocating us. They're trying to stamp out the unadjusteds entirely."

"They killed my partner in the AlignX protest march," Claus says.

Jesus Christ. Hal remembers that rally. It seemed the whole city was marching for LGBTQ+ rights that day. But then the army came out. And so many were injured and killed.

"Intel tells us President Bear plans to make an announcement soon," Matt says. "We expect it will be about an enforced nanite program of some kind."

The hairs on the back of Hal's neck stand tall. Enforced? He can't have a gene-altering pill forced on Mara and Brandon that could end up killing them.

As Hal makes his way home, he can't stop thinking about the meeting. The offers to help. The hope in Matt's voice. Mara is asleep when he gets back, but he's way too wired to join her. Next time he'll bring her. She'll be up for it. She's always so passionate about human rights. Once she sees she's not alone, Hal knows she'll get on board. But then there is Brandon to consider. If they both throw themselves into a highly illegal resistance and something happens to them...

Hal shakes his head. He is a bulk. Nothing will happen to him. He's practically immortal. And that means he's more than capable of keeping Mara and Brandon safe.

At the kitchen table, Hal stares at his computer. An ad for NanoTech scrolls across his screen: *This week only—nanites at unbeatable prices! Perfect enhancements! Lifetime guarantee!* He shivers, half expecting an agent from the NRA to knock on the door.

Is he really ready to drop everything and run? This isn't a game anymore. This is happening. People will get hurt. Worse.

He scrubs his hands over his face. If they stay, they're in Bear's world. If they go, they're in hiding. They can't have it both ways, and neither feels right.

CHAPTER 4

HAL STANDS at the kitchen counter, slicing vegetables for Brandon's dinner, when the doorbell rings. Not the melodic chime he programmed last week, but a harsh, insistent buzz that suggests someone's leaning on it. He sets down the knife, wipes his hands on a dishtowel, and glances at the security screen beside the refrigerator. The image makes him pause —Joe Rucker, all eight feet of him, hunched at the door like he's trying to make himself smaller.

"Mara," Hal calls as he heads toward the door, "Joe's here." Behind him, he hears Brandon's delighted squeal from the living room, followed by Mara's gentle shushing.

When Hal opens the door, the full impact of Joe's presence hits him. The former football player's armored skin catches the fading sunlight. His corn-colored hair is longer than Hal remembers, hanging limply over eyes that seem sunken into his broad face. The cleft in his chin deepens as he attempts a smile.

"Hey," Joe says, like he's not sure he's supposed to be here, and Hal pulls him inside, eyes catching on Joe's stiff and awkward walk. He injured his knee during a game six months ago, and his contract didn't include a regeneration nanite.

They spoke about it all on the phone, but seeing him now, an up-and-coming star cut off, months of rehab, a noticeable limp in his leg...Hal's heart bleeds for his friend.

"You look like hell," Hal says, because it's true and because they've never been the type to dance around things.

"Feel worse." Joe's laugh is hollow as he dumps his duffel bag on the hall floor. "Thanks for having me, buddy."

Hal pats his shoulder. "Anytime, pal."

Joe's gaze falls to Brandon and Mara in the living room, Brandon staring up at Joe with big brown eyes.

"Joe, meet Brandon and Mara," Hal introduces them, nodding first to his son, then his wife. "Guys, this is Joe."

"Nice to meet you both," Joe says, crouching to be at eye level with Brandon, who hides his face in his mother's neck. Mara smiles and touches Joe's arm, welcoming him into the home.

"Sorry about the mess," Mara says, gesturing to the scattered toys and crayon drawings that adorn the living room floor.

Joe waves away the apology. "Looks lived in. It's nice."

Hal leads Joe to the kitchen where they share a beer.

"How did the presentation go?"

Joe looks at the condensation dripping down his beer. "Regeneration nanite denied. I'm disabled for life. Or I figure out a way to pay for one myself."

Hal's gut clenches. Joe is no better off than Miller or Jackson.

"The worst part," Joe continues, his voice dropping so low that Hal has to lean forward to hear him, "is how they look at me now. The team doctors, the coaches, even the fans. Like I'm some broken toy, not worth fixing." He looks up, meeting Hal's eyes. "They called me a 'failed investment' right to my face, Hal. Like I wasn't even in the room."

Bile rises in Hal's throat. How many families will they do this to, leaving people like Joe to fend for themselves the second they fall out of favor? He doesn't have to guess. If they can leave Joe like this, if they can ignore him and his family and leave them out in the cold, how long before it's Hal and Mara and Brandon?

He remembers the hostility Mara faced at The Helix Lounge, the way people dismissed her as something primitive, less evolved. Now Joe, with all his enhancements, is experiencing the same dehumanization from the other side.

"We're going to find you a way out of this," Hal says. That's why he joined the resistance. This isn't just about him and his family. This is the biggest thing he's ever been part of. And the most important.

Joe shrugs his massive shoulders, the movement oddly delicate. "It's legal. Their lawyers made sure of that. And now I'm just another broken bulk with a useless enhancement." He gestures at his enormous body. "All this strength, and I can barely walk some days."

"This isn't the end." Hal remembers the early days, when nanites first hit the market. The promise of a better, stronger, more capable humanity. What no one talked about were the side effects, the incompatibilities, the unforeseen consequences of rewriting human DNA.

"How can it not be?"

Hal leans forward. "There are people who can help. People who are tired of being treated like they're less than human. Whether they're unadjusted or failed altereds."

Joe takes a long sip of his beer. "What kind of people?"

Mara appears in the doorway. "Brandon's asleep," she says. Her eyes move from Hal to Joe, reading the tension. "I'll give you two some space."

"No," Hal says quickly. "Stay, Mara. This concerns you too."

She nods and joins them, sitting beside Hal at the table. She holds his hand.

Mara has been to a couple of meetings now too. The group grows every time. They've had to split into different groups to accommodate the thousands meeting across Central City. They even took Brandon once and his presence seemed to stir passion in the chests of the unadjusteds. And Hal's.

"They're calling us 'regression cases,'" Joe says. "As if we've somehow failed to use our enhancements properly." His laugh is hollow. "The Titans' team doctor actually suggested I should have anticipated the knee injury and compensated with my enhanced reflexes."

"That's ridiculous," Mara says, a rare flash of anger coloring her voice. "No one can predict something like that."

"It's about absolving responsibility," Hal says, the realization settling heavy in his stomach. "If it's your fault for not using your enhancement correctly, then it's not the system's problem when things go wrong."

Joe nods. "Exactly. And now that I'm damaged goods, I'm seeing how thin the veneer of acceptance really was. Same doctors who used to fawn over my 'perfect bulk transformation' now look at me like I'm defective merchandise."

Hal feels the pit in his stomach growing deeper. He's always known the system was unequal—his relationship with Mara has shown him that daily—but what Joe describes is something more insidious. A society actively engineering itself to eliminate those who don't conform, whether by choice or circumstance.

"You mentioned a group of unadjusteds?" Joe asks, breaking Hal out of his thoughts.

Bring friendlies.

Joe is a hell of a friendly.

"Unadjusteds are meeting," Hal says. "They're assigning safe houses. Figuring out underground medical care for altereds with enhancement complications the system won't treat. Information sharing about which companies still hire unadjusteds, which doctors treat everyone equally."

"What about—?"

"A resistance?" Hal nods and Joe's eyebrows shoot up. "Things are moving faster than you might realize. There are already thousands in Central City alone. And some of them are just like us. They're marking hideouts, gathering supplies, weapons—"

"Holy..." Joe trails off. "And you're part of it?"

Hal glances at Mara. "We've been to a couple meetings."

"Things are snowballing fast," Mara says.

"They say something is coming," Hal says. "Some kind of mandate from President Bear. And the unadjusteds are getting ready act. The group is run by this teacher, an ex-karate champion, and a teenager called Matt Lawson."

Joe nods. "Excuse me one sec." He pulls out his phone and steps into the hallway. Hal can only hear Joe's side of the conversation.

"Mom? It's Joe. Just wanted to check in, make sure you and Dad are alright."

Hal exchanges a look with Mara, then grabs a couple of fresh beers from the fridge.

"Yeah, Mom, I'm good. Staying with a friend. Listen, there's talk going around about a resistance against the enhancements. You guys keep your ears open, alright? Stay safe."

Hal uncaps the beers.

"You think he's up for it?" Mara whispers.

"I'm sure," Hal whispers back. "He's been treated like shit."

"Not everyone who's experienced an injustice feels as passionate about a rebellion," Mara replies dryly.

Hal chuckles. "Trust me. He's in."

"Will do, Mom. Love you." Joe finishes his call, then walks back into the living room.

"Everything alright back home?" Hal asks.

"Seems to be," Joe replies. "For now, anyway."

"Good," Hal says firmly, pushing the fresh beer into Joe's hand. "That's good."

"I'm so sorry this has happened to you," Mara says to Joe.

"They throw these nanites at people and then run when it's time to deal with the consequences."

Joe shrugs. "I made the choice to take it."

"But no one knows how it's going to take," Hal says. "And no one really knows the extent of a bulk's strength either."

"Like Ellis," Joe says.

"Ellis," Hal repeats, the name a weight between them. The ghost of their friend seems to materialize—another eight-foot bulk, another transformation, another warning of all that can go wrong in their carefully engineered society.

Mara's hand tightens around Hal's. "I should check on Brandon," she says quietly, understanding this is a conversation the two men need to have alone. As she rises, she touches Joe's shoulder gently. "I'm sorry about Ellis. He was a good man."

Joe nods, his massive hand engulfing hers for a moment. "One of the best."

When Mara disappears, a heavy silence falls between Hal and Joe. Ellis Santiago had been their friend for years. They both knew him from the football circuit, pre-pro training camps. Was tapped to play for the California Vultures.

"I visited his parents last month," Joe finally says. "They still have his room exactly like it was. All his football trophies. His acceptance letter to the academy. Even that ridiculous poster of President Bear he used to have."

Hal remembers Ellis' enthusiasm for the president whose policies had made nanites more accessible, though not truly affordable, to the middle class.

"How are they doing?" Hal asks.

Joe shakes his head. "Not good. Still in debt from the nanite. No compensation from the manufacturer, of course. "Known risks," and all that legal bullshit."

Like Joe, Ellis had seen the bulk nanite as his ticket out of obscurity. A way to transform not just his body but his entire future. Unlike Joe, whose parents had sacrificed everything for his enhancement, Ellis had taken out predatory loans, believing his eventual sports contract would make the financial risk worthwhile.

"Remember how excited he was?" Joe's voice softens with the memory. "Counting down the days until he could afford that pill."

"The day he took it," Hal says, "he called me right before. Said he wanted someone to know exactly when his new life began."

The reality of enhancement had been both more and less than the advertisements promised. Ellis' transformation was spectacular—eight feet of perfectly sculpted muscle, skin like armor, strength that could bend steel. Everything the brochures promised. What they didn't mention were the complications.

Within ten minutes he was dead. "Foamed out," they said. Body didn't take to the change. It happens sometimes. Rarely, but enough to make every potential bulk second guess their decision.

"Did they ever determine exactly what went wrong?" Hal asks, though he's heard the explanation before. He needs to hear it again, to remind himself of the stakes.

Joe's expression darkens. "Officially? 'Genetic incompatibility with class 10 adjustments.' Like it was his fault his

DNA didn't play nice with their nanite." He shakes his head. "Unofficially? The batch was rushed. Three other bulks from the same production run died that year."

"Fucking nanites," Hal says quietly.

"But we still have choices," Joe says.

He meets Joe's eyes and raises his beer in a silent toast. "We do indeed."

CHAPTER 5

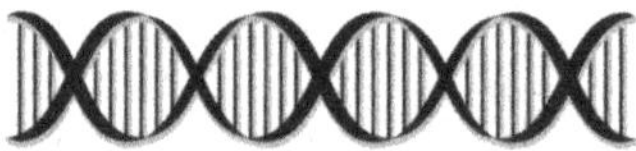

THE PRESIDENTIAL SEAL fills the TV screen. Hal sits up straight, a chill running through his body. Is this the announcement they've been waiting for?

"We interrupt your regularly scheduled programming for an announcement from President Bear," the reporter's voice declares, artificially smooth and perfectly modulated.

Hal's stomach knots. The last time President Bear made an emergency announcement, he called it the Public Health Optimization Drive and encouraged unadjusted citizens to undergo baseline nanite testing to assist in national health surveillance. Everyone knew the word *encouraged* was just a euphemism.

On screen, the presidential seal dissolves, revealing President Bear standing at a podium emblazoned with the national crest. Hal's breath catches. The President's transformation grows more pronounced each time he appears in public. His shoulders have broadened to an inhuman width, stretching his custom suit to its limits. Thick stubble peppers his jawline, no doubt a side effect of his grizzly bear nanite. His red irises gleam unnaturally under the studio lights, and when he grips the podium, Hal notices the faint shimmer of silken webbing between his fingers.

"Good afternoon, my fellow Americans," President Bear begins, his voice a deep rumble that seems to vibrate through the television speakers. It's a voice engineered to command attention, to make listeners stand at attention. Hal involuntarily straightens his posture.

He reaches for his phone, fingers hovering over Mara's contact. She needs to hear this, but he hesitates, wanting to learn what this is about first.

"Today marks a pivotal moment in our nation's history," President Bear continues, displaying that politician's smile that never reaches his eyes. "For too long, we have allowed personal choice to dictate our national security strategy. For too long, we have permitted individuals to remain unadjusted while our global competitors enhance their populations." He pauses, letting his gaze sweep across the camera lens, creating the unsettling impression that he's looking directly at Hal.

"All unadjusteds age twelve and over will now be required to take a nanite pill to enhance their abilities," President Bear declares, his voice dropping an octave. "With threats and competition from overseas, we must do more to further the strength of our country."

Hal's phone slips from his fingers, clattering on the hardwood floor. Mara. Brandon. His entire body goes cold, then hot, then cold again. Mara's office is across town. Brandon's daycare is in the opposite direction. His mind races with calculations.

On screen, President Bear gestures, and a holographic map appears beside him, showing red dots appearing simultaneously across the country.

"The Nanite Representative Agency is on its way to every school right now," President Bear continues, his tone leaving no room for debate. "They will assign each eligible unadjusted a ticket number. You are not permitted to leave before you have your ticket. This ticket will tell you which day within the next two weeks you will be assessed for an appropriate nanite level. You'll notice some of those assessments start today..."

Hal picks up the distant sound of helicopter rotors. It's already starting. This is the announcement Matt and Francesca were talking about. They must both be watching this now too. Matt's probably at school.

The screen splits to show footage that Hal recognizes immediately. Margaret Melody—one of the original creators of the nanite technology—being dragged from her laboratory two years ago. Her lab coat torn, her glasses askew, screaming about rights and choices as armored officers with visible enhancements force her into a government vehicle.

"This is what happens to those who obstruct progress," President Bear says, his voice overlaying the silent footage. "Dr. Melody chose treason over patriotism. She chose to withhold her brilliance from her country when we needed it most."

Margaret Melody is in prison, was found guilty of treason. No parole.

The footage shifts to show gleaming facilities with smiling citizens lining up to receive their nanite assessments.

Everyone looks impossibly happy, impossibly healthy. It's propaganda so blatant it would be laughable if the stakes weren't so high.

"Once this assessment is complete," President Bear continues, his voice pulling Hal back to the immediate threat, "we will proceed to residences to evaluate the unadjusted adults. I expect each unadjusted individual to join the strength of the adjusted superbeings. Failure to comply will result in unfortunate circumstances."

The camera zooms in on President Bear's face, his inhuman red irises whirring with purpose.

The broadcast cuts back to the presidential seal as an automated voice begins listing instructions for the nanite assessment procedures.

Hal lurches to his feet, knocking over the coffee table. He scrabbles for his phone, hands trembling.

He calls Mara's cell first, pacing the living room in tight circles.

"The number you are trying to reach is unavailable. Please try—"

He ends the call with a frustrated growl. Of course. Everyone is calling everyone right now. He tries her direct line.

"This extension is temporarily unavailable—"

"Damn it!" He slams his fist against the wall, leaving a dent in the plaster. Brandon is his priority.

Hal grabs his keys and jacket, mind racing through contingency plans they'd only half-seriously discussed. The cave through the Great Woods. The hidden storage unit with emergency supplies. The contacts who can provide untraceable transportation. All those paranoid preparations he hadn't taken seriously.

He eyes Joe's duffle poking out of the spare room. Hal has no idea where his friends is. And he can't wait for him. He sends him the coordinates to the cave and prays he makes it.

Hal catches a notification on his phone screen, a message from the Reapers' coach: EMERGENCY TEAM MEETING. ALL PLAYERS REPORT IMMEDIATELY.

Hal ignores it. His team, his career, his fame—none of it matters now. Only Mara and Brandon. Only getting them somewhere safe before the nanite representatives come knocking on their door with their tickets and their assessments and their *unfortunate circumstances.*

The television continues droning instructions as Hal rushes out the door. The summer heat hits his face, a humid soup he struggles to inhale. Outside is a cloud of chaos. Three doors down, the Mitchells—fully unadjusted—throw suitcases into their 4x4. Across the street, Mrs. Paxton stands on her porch, the decorative feathers sprouting from her shoulders ruffled in agitation as she speaks urgently into her phone.

"—come home now—" and "—they're really doing it this time—"

The air thrums with tension, a city collectively holding its breath before the scream.

Hal sprints to his car. His phone buzzes continuously in his pocket—team notifications, news alerts, emergency broadcasts—but he ignores them all.

He tries Mara again as he slides behind the wheel. Straight to voicemail.

"Mara, it's me. Don't go anywhere. Don't let anyone give you a ticket. I'm getting Brandon and coming for you. Keep your phone on." His voice cracks slightly. "I love you."

The car roars to life, and Hal peels out of the driveway, tires squealing against the asphalt. The main street of his suburb comes into view, and with it, the first real signs of a city unraveling. The traffic lights still work, but no one heeds them. Cars jam the intersections, horns blaring in a dissonant chorus of panic.

A group of teenagers block the road ahead, their school backpacks abandoned on the sidewalk. One boy, no more than fifteen, displays a fresh pair of antlers sprouting from his temples. He's screaming at an unadjusted girl, her face contorted in defiance.

"It's happening now!" the boy shouts. "Just take the pill! They're coming for you anyway!"

"I won't!" she screams back. "My body, my choice!"

Hal swerves around them, catching a glimpse of two police officers approaching, both bulks. The girl spots them and bolts down an alley.

At the next intersection, a delivery truck has overturned, spilling packages across the road. People scavenge through the contents, grabbing items with unrestrained frenzy. What the hell do they want Ketchup packets for?

Hal navigates through the streets, using side roads when possible, forcing his way through obstructions when necessary.

His phone rings. Unknown number.

"Hello? Mara?" Hal answers, hope surging in his chest.

"Hal Small?" A male voice, unfamiliar. "This is Coach

Decker's office. Your presence is required immediately at Reapers headquarters. Failure to report will be considered—"

Hal ends the call. The Reapers, his teammates, his career...none of it matters now. In his rearview mirror, a pillar of black smoke rises from a building. Someone has started a fire, whether in protest or panic, he can't tell.

Downtown looms ahead, the skyscrapers reflecting the late morning sun. Between Hal and Brandon's daycare lies the heart of the financial district, a place dominated by the enhanced elite.

A woman with bioluminescent skin patterns staggers along the sidewalk, her lights flashing erratically instead of in the usual controlled patterns. Her movements are jerky, uncoordinated, as if she's losing control of her nervous system. Nearby, a man with scaled arms lunges at a passerby, hissing like the reptile whose DNA he shares. Two business executives with identical cranial bulges circle each other in the middle of the street, their faces twisted in mutual hostility.

The threat of violence seeps through the streets. *Altered* violence.

A massive crash sounds as Hal approaches the central business district. Ahead, a bulk soldier is yelling at people cowering behind dumpsters and digiboards. He picks up a car and throws it into a storefront, shattering glass and triggering alarms. People scatter, screaming. The path to Brandon's daycare is now blocked by debris and panicked people trying to get out of the path of destruction.

"No, no, no," Hal mutters, slamming his palm against the

steering wheel. He abandons the car, leaving it haphazardly at the curb.

He weaves through panicked pedestrians, his body automatically adjusting to avoid collisions. The crowds thicken as he approaches the blockage caused by the bulk's breakdown. People push and shove, a mix of adjusted and unadjusted, elbowing each other out the way to climb over the smashed vehicle and jagged debris.

"Make way!" Hal shouts, using the voice that commands attention on the playing field. Some recognize him and step aside. Others, too lost in their own panic, ignore him.

A woman with butterfly wings flutters above the crowd, her eyes scanning for something or someone. Her wings beat erratically, lacking their usual grace. "Tommy!" she calls, voice breaking. "Tommy, where are you?"

Hal pushes forward. Brandon's daycare is just six blocks ahead.

Hal eyes the wreckage, calculating. He backs up several paces, ignores the stares from those around him, and sprints forward. His legs propel him upward as he leaps over the damaged car, then launches himself over the worst of the debris.

He lands on the other side with a roll that would make his coaches proud, coming up to his feet in one fluid motion, glass tinkling harmless to the tarmac. The crowd here is thinner, most people having retreated from the blockage.

Hal jogs down the street. Brandon's daycare appears ahead—"Little Explorers," with its cheerful sign and primary-colored façade. His heart sinks when he sees the black SUVs parked outside. Government vehicles. But this is daycare.

Not a single child here is over the age of twelve. Why are they here?

He slows his approach, scanning the scene. Children are being loaded into vans. Hal spots two bulks in suits checking tablets by the entrance, and several others watching the perimeter.

He ducks behind a parked car, mind racing. Brandon is only two, too young for mandatory enhancement according to Bear's announcement. But that doesn't mean they won't use him as leverage to ensure Mara's compliance. Or worse, use him to lure in any unadjusted relatives who come to claim him.

A side entrance. There has to be a side entrance. Hal circles the block, keeping the daycare in sight while staying out of view of the officials. He finds a service door near the kitchen. He approaches cautiously, using parked cars and dumpsters as cover.

The door is locked, but that's hardly an obstacle for someone with Hal's strength. He wrenches the handle, feeling the lock mechanism give way with a satisfying crunch. Inside, the kitchen is empty, the staff presumably dealing with the chaos in the main rooms.

Hal moves silently through the building, following the sound of frightened children and stressed adults. He pauses at the corner that leads to the main playroom, peering around carefully.

The scene inside turns his blood to ice. Children are being lined up, their details entered into a tablet by a woman with a nose horn.

"Brandon," Hal whispers, scanning the toddler group. His

son sits on a colorful mat, clutching his favorite dinosaur toy, lower lip trembling as he watches the adults with wide, confused eyes. Hal's heart clenches. Brandon doesn't understand what's happening, only that something is wrong.

A childcare worker stands nearby, clearly distressed but attempting to keep the children calm. Hal recognizes her, Ms. Chen, Brandon's group leader. She's unadjusted, and her face shows the strain of trying to maintain normalcy while undoubtedly worrying about her own fate.

Hal waits until the officials are occupied with an older child, then slips around the corner. He catches Ms. Chen's eye and puts a finger to his lips. Her eyes widen in recognition, then understanding.

Slowly, casually, she moves to stand between Brandon and the officials. Hal crouches low and moves along the wall, using toy shelves as cover. He reaches Brandon, scooping him up in one swift motion.

"Daddy!" Brandon exclaims, too loudly.

"Shh, buddy," Hal whispers, pressing his son close. "We're playing a quiet game, okay?"

A suited man turns. "Hey! You can't—"

Ms. Chen knocks over a bin of blocks, sending them clattering across the floor. It buys Hal precious seconds as he ducks back toward the kitchen.

"Stop him!" someone shouts behind him.

Hal runs, Brandon secure in his arms. His enhanced muscle gives him an edge, but he's still burdened with a toddler. Behind him, heavy footsteps indicate pursuit.

"Daddy, fast!" Brandon says, somehow understanding the urgency even at his young age.

Hal bursts through the kitchen door and back into the alley. A security officer, a bulk, blocks the path to the street.

"Hand over the child, Mr. Small," the man says. "Don't make this more difficult than it needs to be."

Hal shifts Brandon to his hip, freeing one arm. "My son is two years old. He's exempt from the enhancement directive."

"For now," the officer steps forward. "All unadjusteds are being documented. Even if they're under twelve."

That wasn't in President Bear's broadcast. If it had been, the streets would be even more of a mess.

Hal sees the moment the officer intends to make his move. He reacts first, using his free arm to flip a nearby dumpster between them. The heavy metal container crashes down, blocking the alley.

"Hold tight, Brandon," Hal says, then leaps upward, propelling them to the fire escape of the adjacent building. Brandon giggles, thinking it's all a game.

Hal climbs quickly, reaching the roof. From this vantage point, he can see more of the city. Smoke rises from multiple locations now. Above his head, a helicopter circles—military, not news.

He pulls out his phone, trying Mara again while cradling Brandon against his chest.

"Hal?" Her voice fills him with such relief he nearly collapses. "Hal, what's happening? They've locked down the building. No one can leave."

"Listen carefully," he says, scanning the horizon, noting the directions where the chaos seems worst. "I have Brandon. We're coming for you. Don't take any pills. Don't let them process you. Hide if you can."

"They're already in the building, going floor by floor. Oh god, Hal—"

"I'm coming," he promises. "We'll get you out. Just stay safe until we get there."

He ends the call, mind already plotting the fastest route to Mara's office building. The streets below are deteriorating further into chaos. A group of heavily enhanced individuals moves through the streets with military precision. President Bear's bulk army.

CHAPTER 6

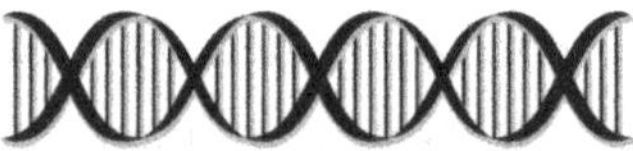

THE AIR TASTES of smoke and fear as Hal clutches Brandon against his armored chest. Around them, sirens wail, people run, glass shatters. Altereds attack in the streets.

Hal watches as two bulks collide near an overturned bus, pavement cracking beneath their boots. One swings a reinforced arm, catching the other across the jaw and sending him crashing into a lamppost, which folds like paper.

Across the intersection, a woman with serpentine reflexes launches herself at a winged teen trying to fly away. She drags him to the ground, wings twisting beneath them. He screams—not in pain, but in fury.

Hal doesn't understand it. These aren't random acts of violence. *They're targeting each other.* Enhanced against enhanced.

That wasn't in President Bear's announcement.

He watches as another group of altereds, a trio with glowing eyes and synchronized movement, descends on a young girl as she straightens her ripped shirt. *She doesn't even have time to scream.*

Something is wrong. *Deeply wrong.*

Hal picks out the fine tremors in their movements—the glitchy stutters, the erratic spasms, pupils blown wide. *They're not in control.*

He's heard stories about this at the resistance meetings. The "overload effect." Too much enhancement. Too much animal DNA. Enhanced humans who have taken multiple nanites need regular contact with unenhanced humans to maintain psychological stability. Something about baseline human pheromones grounding the altered brain chemistry. The unadjusteds anchoring the adjusteds to their humanity. And now, with the unadjusteds running...there is no one to keep the altereds grounded.

Hal sucks in a breath, checks his own mental state for any hint of anger. Feels a dull rage, but it's directed at President Bear, not any of the people fighting in the streets.

A hulking man stumbles into an alley, pounding his fists against his own skull as if trying to silence something screaming inside. Behind him, an altered with chameleon skin flickers between visibility and static-like shimmer, convulsing with every step.

"Are they...sick?" Brandon whispers, eyes wide.

Hal doesn't answer. He doesn't know what to call it.

Drones fly overhead. Gunfire sounds in the street. The army marches closer.

Mara. He has to reach her.

"Daddy," Brandon whimpers, his small fingers gripping Hal's arms. "Loud."

"I know, buddy." Hal adjusts his hold, cradling Brandon's head against his shoulder to muffle the sounds. "Just a little longer."

He steps into the street where overturned vehicles burn, thankful for his fire-retardant skin. A chunk of concrete sails through the air toward them. Hal swivels, presenting his broad back to absorb the impact. It cracks against his shoulder blades, crumbling into dust. Brandon doesn't feel the hit, but he senses his father's movement.

"Are we flying?" the toddler asks, his voice small and hopeful.

"Not today, buddy," Hal says, managing a smile despite the circumstances. "Daddy can't fly, remember? Just really strong."

A roadblock appears ahead, a makeshift barricade where a squad of men in black tactical gear check IDs. They're separating people into two lines. Hal doesn't need enhanced hearing to understand what's happening. Those with visible modifications pass through easily. Those without are detained.

"Designation check!" A guard spots Hal's approach, raising a scanner.

Hal stops, allowing the device to read his biometrics. The scanner beeps green.

"Class ten bulk enhancement," the guard says, eyeing Hal with respect. "You're clear to proceed, sir." His gaze drops to Brandon. "Is the child enhanced?"

Hal's jaw clenches. "He's two years old."

The guard's expression hardens. "Policy requires verification of all individuals. Current unadjusted protocols—"

"He's my *son*," Hal cuts him off, voice low and dangerous.

The guard steps back, hand moving to his weapon. But a gun can't kill a bulk. Not really. Other personnel turn their attention toward the confrontation.

Brandon begins to cry. "Daddy, scary man."

Something in his son's voice, the pure, unfiltered fear, breaks through the standoff. The guard's eyes flicker between Hal and his son.

"Move along," he finally says, waving them through. "But if you're harboring unmodified adults, that's on your head."

Hal doesn't respond, simply strides through the gap they create for him. Once past the checkpoint, he whispers reassurances to Brandon, whose tears are already drying.

"Good boy," Hal says. "You're so brave, just like Mommy."

At the mention of Mara, Brandon brightens. "Mommy story?"

Despite everything, Hal smiles. Even now, their ritual. "Once upon a time," he begins, walking steadily through the chaos, "there was a beautiful princess named Mara who fell in love with a very lucky ogre named Hal."

"Not ogre," Brandon giggles. "Bulk!"

"That's right, a bulk. And they loved each other very much, even though some people thought they shouldn't be together."

Hal's narrative provides comfort to them both as they navigate the increasingly hostile streets. Inside, his heart pounds with fear for Mara.

Mara's office building houses primarily traditional businesses that employ unadjusteds in clerical positions. Exactly the kind of place nanite reps would target.

Three blocks from their destination, the sound of footsteps behind him makes Hal spin around. Three figures lurch out of an alley—civilian clothes, but carrying military-grade weapons. One has horns, another teleports three feet closer, the third lets out a scream that shatters windows. Altereds. All three of them. Gone crazy. They can't be reasoned with.

Hal turns to run.

The teleporter flashes in front of him. "Where you going in such a hurry?"

Hal backs away slowly. "Just taking my son to safety."

All three of them look at Brandon. There is no sympathy in their eyes, only violence.

Hal moves without thinking, tucking Brandon tighter against his chest and charging forward. He throws out a fist and catches the teleporter across the jaw before the guy can block his path.

A shot pings off his shoulder. The second hits his thigh. Neither penetrates.

Hal barrels into them like a freight train. He sends the guy with horns flying against the wall with a sickening crunch. The screamer raises his weapon to fire at point-blank range, but Hal's fist connects first, crushing the rifle barrel and the hand holding it.

The alley falls silent except for Brandon's muffled crying and Hal's heavy breathing.

"Shh, it's okay," Hal soothes, checking Brandon for injuries. "We're okay."

He steps over the bodies, forcing himself not to think about what just happened. What he just did. There will be time for that later. Right now, getting to Mara is all that matters.

When they finally emerge onto the street that houses Mara's office building, Hal's heart sinks. The elegant glass tower is surrounded by military vehicles. Soldiers stand in formation, weapons trained on the entrance. Others move methodically floor by floor, visible through the building's transparent exterior.

A crowd of altered spectators has gathered behind the military cordon, watching the operation with expressions ranging from grim satisfaction to outright glee.

"Sir, you can't go any further." A soldier steps into Hal's path, palm raised.

Hal scans the building for Mara. Third floor, east side. Her office window. There—movement. Figures in tactical gear entering her department.

"My wife works in there," Hal says, desperation creeping into his voice. "She's on the third floor."

The soldier's expression softens. "I'm sorry, but all unadjusteds are being processed according to the new protocols." He glances at Brandon. "Is the child—"

"He's with me," Hal cuts him off, unwilling to have this conversation again.

A commotion erupts at the building's entrance as a group of unadjusteds is marched out at gunpoint. Hal scans their faces frantically, equal parts relieved and dismayed when Mara isn't among them.

"Look, I understand your concern," the soldier says, lowering his voice. "But you need to understand what's happening. With the unadjusteds refusing to conform, they're being rounded up and taken to processing centers."

"What kind of processing centers?" Hal asks, the words like ash in his mouth.

The soldier doesn't answer, which is answer enough.

Hal shifts Brandon to his other arm, the boy now quiet. "I need to get to her."

"That's not possible, sir. Even for you." Recognition shines in the soldier's eyes, but it doesn't stop his hand dropping to his sidearm. Hal could take him out. But there are a shit ton of bulk soldiers here and he can't take them all on with Brandon in his arms. "I suggest you take your son somewhere safe. This area is going to be restricted for several hours."

Through the glass façade, Hal watches soldiers kick down doors on the third floor. He zeroes in on Mara's office section.

There she is. Mara. Standing tall despite the fear that must be coursing through her. Her hands are raised as armed men surround her and her coworkers. Even from this distance, even through the glass and chaos, her eyes find his. Recognition. Love. Fear.

"Stand back," Hal tells the soldier, his voice deadly quiet. "I'm going in there."

"That's not happening," the soldier replies, drawing his weapon fully now. "Stand down, or we'll consider you hostile."

More soldiers notice the confrontation, turning their attention toward Hal. Weapons raise. Warning shouts echo.

Brandon whimpers, clinging tighter to his father's neck. "Daddy, I'm scared."

The sound of his son's voice cuts through Hal's fury. He can't risk Brandon. Not even for Mara.

Through the glass walls, he sees Mara mouthing something to him.

"Keep him safe."

Hal stands at the perimeter, his son in his arms, his wife within sight but unreachable, as the world they've built together balances on the edge of destruction. Soldiers advance toward the building entrance, weapons ready, while inside, the sweep continues floor by floor.

"Let me through," Hal pleads, one final attempt. "She's my wife."

"Rules are rules," the soldier replies. "If she cooperates, there is nothing to worry about."

Hal stares up at the third floor, at Mara's resolute face among her frightened colleagues. Brandon follows his gaze, spotting his mother.

"Mommy!" he cries, waving his small hand. "Mommy!"

Behind the soldier, a line of unadjusteds stumbles out of the building, hands zip-tied behind their backs. Their faces bear the blank shock of people whose worlds have collapsed in minutes. An older woman trips, falling to her knees. When she can't rise fast enough, a soldier casually raises his rifle and fires. The sound is oddly muffled—suppressed weapons, designed for urban operations.

The woman crumples. No one helps her. No one even seems surprised.

"Daddy, lady fell down," Brandon whispers, his voice small against Hal's neck.

Hal covers his son's eyes. "Don't look, buddy."

Hal closes his eyes briefly, collecting himself. Then, cradling Brandon securely against his chest, he steps back, calculating. The soldiers relax, thinking he's giving up.

They don't realize what a bulk is capable of when protecting his family.

Through the glass walls, he watches Mara being forced to her knees alongside other unadjusteds from her office. The soldiers' movements are methodical, practiced, as if they've rehearsed this day for months. Perhaps they have.

Hal backs away from the checkpoint, mind racing. There must be another entrance, a service door, something. He scans the building's exterior, mapping potential entry points. The loading dock? Too heavily guarded. The emergency exits? Alarmed and watched.

Brandon whimpers. Hal strokes his son's back. He hates that Brandon has to witness this, that his young mind will carry these memories.

A sudden commotion draws his attention back to the third floor. Soldiers are separating the unadjusteds into groups. Some are forced toward the elevators. Others, including Mara, remain kneeling on the ground.

Hal doesn't need to be told what this selection means.

He moves without conscious thought, pushing past onlookers, calculating trajectories and forces. If he can reach the north side of the building, he might be able to scale the exterior. His enhancements allow him to punch handholds into concrete. Three floors is nothing with his strength.

But Brandon—what about Brandon? He can't climb with his son in his arms, can't risk him falling. Yet there's no one he trusts to take him, nowhere safe to leave him.

A sharp crack echoes, followed by screams from the crowd. Hal turns to see another wave of unadjusteds being marched from the building. This time, there's no pretense of processing. Soldiers open fire, dropping unadjusteds where they stand. Bodies crumple onto the plaza, blood pooling on polished stone.

The spectators retreat in surprise, not at the killings but at the public nature of the execution. Some record the scene with their phones, footage that will no doubt be shared across networks with approving commentary.

"This is what happens to genetic purists," a man beside Hal says, his voice thick with satisfaction. "Should have enhanced when they had the chance."

Hal's armored fist twitches with the desire to crush the man's throat. But Brandon's weight in his arms grounds him. *Focus. Get to Mara.*

He makes his decision. The main entrance is lightly guarded now that most soldiers are occupied with the executions. If he moves fast enough, uses his bulk strength...

"Hold on tight, Brandon," he whispers. "We're going to run really fast to get Mommy."

Brandon nods against his chest, tiny fingers gripping Hal's collar. "Fast like when you play ball?"

"Even faster." Hal kisses his son's forehead, feeling the soft, vulnerable skin against his lips. Then he runs.

The world blurs around him as he accelerates. Soldiers turn too slowly, their weapons tracking empty air where he was a split second before.

Fifty yards to the entrance. Forty. Thirty.

A high-velocity round strikes the pavement near his feet.

Another whistles past his ear. They're leading their shots now, adjusting for his speed. And the vulnerable holes in the back of his neck and both knees. Smart.

Twenty yards. The glass doors loom ahead, shattered in several places.

A shout goes up—"Bulk incoming!"—and weapons swivel toward him.

Something hits Hal's back with the force of a hammer blow. His armored skin absorbs it. Another shot pings off his shoulder.

Ten yards. Almost there.

The world slows to a crawl. Hal sees everything with crystalline clarity—the soldiers adjusting their aim, the frightened faces of the crowd, the blinking red lights of security systems activating building lockdown.

And then—the whine of a high-powered rifle. Different from the others. Higher pitch. Meant to destroy.

Hal turns, trying to shield Brandon with his body.

Too late.

The round punches through the air, a barely visible streak of death. It strikes not Hal's skin, but the small, vulnerable body in his arms.

Brandon jerks once, a tiny gasp escaping his lips. His eyes widen, more in surprise than pain.

"Daddy?" he whispers.

Blood blooms across the front of his dinosaur T-shirt, spreading with impossible speed. Too much blood for such a small body.

"No," Hal breathes. "*No, no, no.*"

He skids to a halt, cradling Brandon in his arms. The

world narrows to his son's face, now ominously pale. The light in his eyes, so bright and curious moments before, flickers like a dying flame.

"Brandon," Hal whispers, his voice failing him. "Stay with me, buddy."

But Brandon's gaze has already gone distant, focusing on something Hal can't see. His small chest rises once, twice, then stills.

The silence that follows is absolute. As if the universe itself has paused to witness this unbearable moment.

Hal sinks to his knees, still holding his son's body. Around him, the roundup continues—shouting, gunfire, screams. None of it penetrates the bubble of grief enclosing him and Brandon.

He touches his son's cheek, still warm.

A soldier approaches cautiously, weapon trained on Hal. "Sir, put the child down and step away."

Hal doesn't look up. Can't look away from Brandon's face, so peaceful it might be sleeping if not for the crimson stain spreading across his chest.

"Sir, I won't ask again." The soldier's voice wavers as his eyes fall on the tiny, broken body.

Hal's gaze finally lifts, and whatever the soldier sees in his eyes makes him step back.

"Get away from me," Hal says.

The soldier retreats, signaling to his team to back up. Even in their cruelty, they recognize the danger of cornering a predator with nothing left to lose.

A movement in the corner of Hal's vision draws his attention upward. Third floor. Mara's office.

She stands at the window, hands pressed against the glass. She saw what happened. Her face contorts in a silent scream, her body straining toward them as if she could break through the barriers by will alone.

A soldier grabs her, dragging her back from the window. She fights wildly, all composure gone. Her mouth forms one word, over and over: "Brandon!"

Hal rises to his feet, his son's body cradled against his chest, suddenly light as air. He takes a step toward the building, then another. Soldiers move to intercept him, but something in his posture makes them hesitate.

Mara struggles against her captors, her eyes never leaving Hal. Another soldier approaches, shouting something at her. She spits in his face.

The soldier raises his weapon.

"No!" Hal roars, the sound tearing from his throat with such force that windows vibrate. He lunges forward, but strong hands grab him from behind.

He watches, helpless, as the soldier on the third floor places his weapon against Mara's temple. Her eyes find Hal's one last time. Her lips move.

"I love you."

The muzzle flash is small, almost insignificant. Mara crumples, disappearing from view below the window line.

Something breaks inside Hal, something fundamental and irreparable. With a growl, Hal throws off his captors. Some fly through the air and crumple against walls. Others draw weapons, opening fire at point-blank range.

The bullets strike Hal's armored skin and ricochet away.

One finds a soldier's unprotected face. Another punctures the battery of a military vehicle, exploding it into the air.

Hal cradles his dead son in one arm, his free hand crushing a soldier's weapon—and the hand holding it—into unrecognizable pulp.

In the space of minutes, he has lost everything that anchored him to humanity. His wife. His child. His future.

Around him, the roundup continues. Unadjusteds lined up for execution. Enhanced civilians watching with approval or indifference. Military efficiency in service of genocide.

Hal looks down at Brandon's still face, then up at the window where he last saw Mara. The world has taken everything from him. What will he take from the world in return?

The answer comes with the certainty of a heartbeat: Everything.

But not here. And not now.

He turns and walks away.

CHAPTER 7

HAL RUNS through the empty streets of Central City, his son's body cradled against his chest.

Brandon weighs nothing in his bulk-enhanced arms, a terrible lightness that makes Hal's stomach clench. The boy's curls flutter with each step, almost as if he's just sleeping, but the stillness tells Hal what he can't bear to acknowledge. Darkness rolls between the skyscrapers, shrouding the city in a gloom that matches the emptiness spreading through Hal's chest.

"I'm taking you somewhere better," Hal whispers, his voice cracking as he cuts through an alley between two gleaming towers.

He runs for hours. Advertisements featuring the armored physique of bulks loom overhead on digital billboards, smiling faces promising enhancements that will "change your life forever." The irony makes him want to scream.

Hal is turning his back on football. Turning his back on

the city. Turning his back on everything. He'll put his skills to use for the resistance. For Brandon. For Mara.

The city thins as he approaches the eastern limits. Here, the glittering high-rises give way to older buildings with fewer lights, fewer enhancements embedded in their architecture. Hal passes fewer pedestrians, and those he does see have fewer visible alterations. His lungs expand with a hint of relief.

He cuts through a deserted lot, picking his way past the skeleton of an abandoned building project. Brandon's body bounces gently against his chest. Hal tries not to think about how, just yesterday, that same little body had wiggled with energy, demanding "Up, Daddy, up!" and shrieking with delight when Hal hoisted him onto his shoulders.

Ahead, orange lights punctuate the darkness. A checkpoint.

Hal slows his pace, considering his options. His celebrity might get him through, or it might flag extra attention. His bulk enhancement is impossible to hide. He could try to bypass the checkpoint entirely, but enhanced motion sensors and thermal imaging would likely catch him.

Direct approach, then. He adjusts Brandon in his arms, drawing his jacket completely over the boy's face. His heart thuds painfully against his ribcage.

Three soldiers staff the checkpoint, each wearing the red arm bands of the Nanite Enforcement Agency. Their own military-grade alterations are visible in the metallic sheen of their skin and the too-perfect symmetry of their movements. A reinforced barrier spans the road, and a small booth houses scanning equipment.

As Hal approaches, one soldier looks up sharply. Recognition flickers in his expression.

"Identification," the soldier says automatically, then pauses. "Wait—Small? Hal Small? The Reaper?"

Hal nods curtly, shifting Brandon's weight in his arms.

The soldier's demeanor changes instantly, his posture relaxing into the familiar pose of a fan meeting a celebrity. "Man, I can't believe it. I had money on you guys last season. That play against the Metahumans? When you stopped their entire offensive line solo? Legendary."

"Thanks," Hal says, his voice flat. "I need to get through."

The soldier finally notices the bundle in Hal's arms. His eyes narrow. "What've you got there? And where are you headed this late? City is locked down."

"Family emergency," Hal says.

The second soldier approaches, a woman with artificial lenses for eyes, the kind that boost vision and tactical processing. "Protocol requires scanning of all packages and verification of destination, even for persons of note."

"It's not a package," Hal says, his grip tightening instinctively. "It's my son."

The first soldier's expression shifts to confusion. "Your son? But there's no heat signature... Wait." Understanding dawns on his face, followed by an awkward attempt at sympathy. "Oh. I'm sorry, man."

The female soldier shows no such emotion. "Dead or alive, we need to verify. Rules are rules."

"Let me handle this, Vega," the first soldier says, stepping closer to Hal. He lowers his voice. "Look, Mr. Small, I get it. Tough situation. But you know how it is these days—gotta follow protocol. Just let us do a quick scan, verify nothing dangerous, and you can be on your way."

Hal hesitates, then nods stiffly.

The soldier guides him toward the scanner. "You know, someone with your enhancements would be welcome in the NEA. Especially someone with your public profile. We're always looking for bulks. The pay's good, and you'd be helping keep order. Something to think about, maybe after... well, after you deal with your current situation."

Hal says nothing as the scanner's blue light passes over him and Brandon. The soldier continues, seemingly encouraged by Hal's silence.

"Between us," he says, leaning closer, "it's important work we're doing. Making sure people understand that enhancement is the future. That resistance is pointless." He glances at Brandon's covered form. "Did the kid inherit your enhancement?"

"No," Hal says.

The soldier makes a sympathetic clicking sound. "Shame. Those anti-enhancement types don't understand they're condemning their kids to obsolescence. Or worse."

Something snaps inside Hal's chest. A dam breaking, releasing a flood of rage he didn't know was building. He sees red—literally.

"His name was Brandon," Hal says, his voice dangerously quiet.

"Huh?" The soldier looks confused.

"My son. His name was Brandon." Hal carefully places his son's body on the ground, arranging the jacket to fully cover him. "He was two years old. He liked dinosaurs and bananas and splashing in puddles. He was perfect."

The soldier takes a step back, sensing the change in Hal's demeanor. "Look, I didn't mean—"

Hal moves with the explosive speed that made him famous on the field. His fist connects with the soldier's chin before the man can finish his sentence. Despite the soldier's own enhancements, he flies backward, crashing into the barrier control panel in a shower of sparks.

The female soldier—Vega—reacts instantly, her hand moving to her weapon. Hal pivots, grabbing her arm with one hand and lifting her completely off the ground. Her eye lenses may allow her to process situations with rapid speed, but she is no match for a bulk. He tosses her aside like a rag doll, her body slamming into the checkpoint booth.

The third soldier manages to fire a shot. The bullet strikes Hal's chest and flattens against his armored skin, dropping harmlessly to the ground. Hal crosses the distance between them in two strides and delivers an open-palm strike that sends the soldier flying into the darkness beyond the checkpoint's orange lights.

Hal stands in the silence that follows. On autopilot, he strips the largest soldier of his clothing, changes into the uniform. Warmer for the woods, and he might be able to pass for a NEA agent. Then he returns to Brandon, gently lifting his son's body once more.

"I'm sorry you had to see that," he whispers. "I'm sorry for a lot of things."

Hal steps through the damaged barrier, leaving the checkpoint behind. Ahead lies open country, then the vast expanse of the Great Woods. Somewhere in those woods, other unadjusteds are running. If they made it out of the city.

The rage in Hal's chest hardens into something colder, more focused. He adjusts his son's weight one last time and begins to run, carrying them both into the darkness, away from the city that took everything he loved.

✕✕✕✕✕

Dawn breaks over the forgotten cemetery at the edge of the Great Woods, painting the crumbling headstones in pale gold light. Hal stands at the perimeter, Brandon's body still cradled in his arms, taking in the scene. Unlike the perpetual glow of Central City's bright lights, this place exists in natural rhythm, untouched by architectural upgrades. Weeds push through cracked concrete paths, and ancient trees have lifted sections of the wrought iron fence with patient, decades-long persistence. It's beautiful in its imperfection—like Brandon was. Like all unaltered humans are.

Hal steps through a gap in the fence. According to the weathered sign hanging askew at the entrance, this was once the Oakridge Natural Burial Ground, a place where people chose to be interred without preservation enhancements or digital memorials. The kind of place that's becoming increasingly rare as the enhanced majority opt for body preservation or consciousness uploads.

"This is it, buddy," Hal whispers to Brandon, the words catching in his throat. "I think you'll like it here."

He walks between the rows of simple markers, some stone, some wood, all bearing the signs of natural decay.

Names, dates, and sometimes a line of text. Genuine expressions of love from one unadjusted human to another.

Near the back of the cemetery, beneath the spreading branches of the largest oak, Hal finds an empty space. The area feels right somehow. Sheltered, peaceful, with morning light filtering through the leaves to create shifting patterns on the ground. He lays Brandon gently on a bed of fallen leaves and looks around for something to dig with.

Hal spots a rusted shovel leaning against a maintenance shed. It's old and worn, its wooden handle splintering from weather and disuse. He tests its weight, negligible in his enhanced hands, then returns to the spot he's chosen.

The first thrust of the shovel into earth feels like therapy. He could dig the entire grave in minutes if he wanted to, but he deliberately slows himself, turning each shovelful of dirt into a meditation, a final act of care for his son.

"I used to dig holes with you at the park," he says as he works, the pile of earth growing beside him. "Remember that sandbox by the duck pond? You'd get so excited when we hit water." A sad smile touches his lips. "You'd splash it everywhere. Got so mad at me once when I wouldn't let you drink it."

Sweat beads on Hal's forehead. It feels good—human—to exert himself this way, to feel muscle and sinew working for something meaningful rather than for sport or spectacle. Each thrust of the shovel digs not just into earth but into memory: Brandon's first steps, the way he'd say "da-da" with such conviction, his obsession with touching Hal's armored skin and giggling at how it felt.

The grave takes shape. So small. So terribly small. When

it is deep enough, Hal sets the shovel aside and kneels beside Brandon's body. He unwraps the jacket just enough to see his son's face one last time. In death, Brandon looks peaceful, his innocent features relaxed, brown curls framing his face just as they did in life.

"I don't know the right words for this," Hal admits, his voice breaking. "Your mom would. She always knows what to say." He straightens Brandon's dinosaur T-shirt, the cartoon T-Rex on the front covered in dried blood. "I should have protected you better. We should have run a long time ago."

A breath of air flows through the trees, as if the heavens are listening.

"I'm going to fight for you," Hal says. "I'm going to fight for all the unadjusteds."

He rewraps Brandon in the jacket. It's ridiculously large for Brandon's small body, but Hal tucks it around him like a cocoon, as if it could protect his son even now.

"I love you, Brandon," he whispers as he lowers the bundle into the grave. "I'll always love you."

The work of filling the grave is mechanical, each shovelful of dirt landing with terrible finality. Hal moves on autopilot until it's done. Then he fashions a marker from a fallen branch and a piece of his shirt, tearing the fabric and using a sharp stone to carve Brandon's name and the date.

Standing before the small mound of fresh earth, Hal feels the grief transmute into something else, something harder and more focused. The rage that exploded at the checkpoint crystallizes into cold determination.

Hal turns toward the Great Woods stretching beyond the cemetery. With one last look at Brandon's grave, Hal steps into the shadow of the forest. The transition is immediate—from open sky to a cathedral of leaves and branches. Dawn's light filters through in shafts, illuminating patches of fern and moss. The sounds shift too—from distant road noise to the complex symphony of birds, rustling leaves, and small creatures moving through underbrush.

Years of professional football have taught Hal how to read terrain and move efficiently through space. On the field, it was about finding gaps in defensive lines, anticipating movements, maximizing his bulk-enhanced speed and power. Here, those same skills apply. He studies the ground, identifying the firmest path that will leave minimal traces. He scans for low-hanging branches that might scrape against his height. He plots a course.

Hal moves deeper into the woods, his stride lengthening as he finds his rhythm. His thoughts turn to Mara as he runs. The ache in his heart turning hard and cold.

Three miles in, Hal picks up the distinctive whine of helicopter blades. He freezes, dropping into a crouch behind a thick stand of underbrush.

A few minutes later, two soldiers appear. One of them directs a drone. They move in a standard sweep pattern two hundred yards to his right, the drone darting ahead to scan with infrared and motion detection. Military-grade equipment, not the civilian security he encountered at the checkpoint.

Hal analyzes their movement pattern, drawing on years of studying game footage. The patrol is systematic but predictable—the same mistake rookie defenders make when trying to contain veteran runners. They're creating a grid pattern that leaves consistent blind spots.

He waits until the drone moves ahead of the soldiers, then uses his enhanced speed to dash across an open space between two blind spots.

The patrol passes without detecting him. Hal allows himself a grim smile. The same enhancements that made him a sports hero are now helping him become something else—a fugitive, a rebel.

He continues deeper into the forest, where the trees grow taller and the undergrowth thicker. Signs of civilization recede with each mile. Twice more he evades patrols.

By mid-afternoon, Hal notices subtle changes in the forest. Deliberate patterns in the arrangement of fallen logs. Bent branches that might serve as trail markers for those who know how to read them. Small clearings that appear natural but show signs of recent human presence.

He catches a flash of color that doesn't belong—a small strip of blue fabric tied around a tree branch, positioned where it would be visible only from certain angles. Was it left by the resistance?

Hal pauses, studying the marker. This could be random—a hiker's lost bandana—or it could be exactly what he's looking for.

He adjusts his course to follow the direction indicated by the marker. The path grows more difficult, leading up steeper terrain and through denser vegetation. It's the kind of route designed to discourage casual travelers and deter a tail.

As the sun begins to set, Hal crests a ridge and pauses. He finds another marker and turns in the indicated direction.

A hint of a smile breaks out on his face. This is definitely a trail. It will lead him all the way to the cavern. Where he'll formulate a plan of revenge.

Hal has never been a violent man, but the image of strangling President Bear with his own hands refuses to leave his mind. It spurs his steps and his determination. Gives him a reason to live.

CHAPTER 8

FIVE DAYS in the Great Woods turns Hal into something between beast and ghost. He moves with animal instinct through the underbrush, every sense attuned to the patrols that sweep the forest. His skin collects dirt and moss like camouflage. The hunger hollows him, even as the grief does its own carving, sculpting his rage into something cold and purposeful.

Hal tracks the subtle markers left for those who know to look—blue fabric tied to branches and subtle arrows crafted from twigs and twine.

At night, curled beneath fallen logs or in shallow depressions covered with leaves, Hal's dreams are filled with Brandon's laugh, with Mara's smile. He wakes with his son's name on his lips and the phantom weight of a small body in his arms. The memories are like wounds that refuse to scab over, raw and seeping.

On the fifth day, as the afternoon sun filters through the leaves, Hal's hears a sound that doesn't belong—a low, rhythmic clicking. He freezes, pressing himself against the rough bark of an ancient oak. The sound comes again, closer now: the jack of a hammer.

Hal peers around the tree to see a figure materializing from behind a stand of pines, dressed in camouflage that blends seamlessly with the forest. The woman holds a rifle with casual expertise, and Hal recognizes her immediately—Francesca Montoya, one of the resistance leaders.

He steps out. Francesca looks up, rifle raised, then after a few tense seconds, lowers the weapon.

"Small," she says. "Never thought you'd actually show up. You here to join?"

Hal nods.

"This way."

Hal follows her down the bank of a valley and into a small copse of trees. A door appears from nowhere, set into a mound of rock and earth. His heart rate increases. He recognizes excitement rushing through his veins. It's the first time he's felt something other than grief or anger for six days.

Francesca opens the door and gestures for him to follow. They walk along a gradually descending path lit with the occasional lantern. Moisture glistens on the limestone walls. The smell of clay fills his nostrils.

The narrow passage widens into a vast cavern, illuminated by strings of battery-powered lights and lanterns. The underground space hums with low conversations that fall silent as Hal enters.

Matt Lawson steps forward. The last time they met was at a resistance meeting in the city, where Matt had outlined the escape plan if things got worse. Hal hadn't thought he'd need it so soon.

"You made it," Matt says, extending a hand. "You on your own?"

Hal nods, the unspoken words lodging in his throat like stones.

Francesca guides him to a secluded corner where plastic crates serve as makeshift chairs. The three of them sit, and other resistance members give him wary looks. As far as he can tell, he's the only one in the cave with visible enhancements.

"What happened?" Matt asks quietly.

Hal takes a deep breath. "The day of the announcement. Mara was at work. Brandon at daycare. I managed to get to Brandon first. The city was a mess. Altereds killing each other in the streets." His fists clench, the memory fresh despite the days that have passed. "When we finally got to Mara's office, it was surrounded by NEA agents. They wouldn't let anyone in or out. I saw Mara..." His voice breaks. "In the window. Fighting back. They put a bullet in her head." He swallows.

Matt's expression turns grim. "I'm so sorry."

The words come in painful bursts now, each one torn from somewhere deep in his chest. "I tried to run with Brandon, but he was hit by a rogue bullet." He glances at his armored skin. "All this protection and I couldn't save my son."

"It's not your fault," Francesca says. "It's President Bear's. And we're going to make him pay."

More resistance members gather around, their expressions a mixture of sympathy and grim determination. Among them, a young woman with long dark hair and startling green wings approaches. Her emerald eyes fix on Hal with a depth of understanding that catches him off guard.

"I'm Paige," she says. "Paige Starling. My parents were early adopters—started with the health nanites, then got hooked on the cosmetic ones." She gestures to her wings with a sad smile. "I thought these might make them see me, but they were too far gone. Now I fly for the resistance instead."

Something in her gentle candor cracks the ice around Hal's heart. Not healing, not yet, but an acknowledgment that he's not alone in his loss.

"Is there anything left of them?" Hal asks, his voice a rough whisper. "The people who take these pills. Is there any way back?"

A murmur runs through the gathered crowd, and Hal notices the way eyes dart toward a narrow passage he hadn't noticed before.

Matt follows his gaze and nods. "Rufus Melody. Should be arriving soon. We've managed to secure lab equipment. He's our hope for a cure."

Hal startles. "A cure? Is that even possible?"

He looks at his enhanced muscles. What would it be like to not be a bulk? To be unadjusted again?

"We hope," Matt replies. "He created the nanites. We're hoping he can uncreate them."

"And hope is what we fight for." Paige adds, her wings shifting with her breath.

Hal looks around the cavern, taking in the determined faces of the resistance members. He spots a couple more with enhancements. A young woman with purple butterfly wings. A red-haired girl who is over seven feet tall. Seems he's not the only altered unhappy with the nanite mandate.

For the first time since burying Brandon, something besides rage flickers in his chest. It's fragile, this spark, but it's there.

"I want to help," Hal says. "Whatever it takes, I'm in."

"I was hoping you'd say that," Matt says. "We could use your bulk skills."

The next day, Hal stands in the main chamber of the cave during breakfast before the small gathering of resistance members.

"I can't bring back my son," Hal says, determination carrying his voice. "I can't save my wife. But I can put these enhancements to use against the people who forced them on us." He lifts his arms, the muscles rippling beneath his armored skin. "President Bear thinks bulks like me are his perfect soldiers. Let me show him how wrong he is."

Francesca steps forward. "We'll put you to work," she says with a nod. "God knows, we need the muscle."

From the back of the gathering, Claus approaches, leaning on a cane. His blue eyes study Hal with an intensity that feels like being X-rayed.

"You have much anger," Claus says, his German accent lending his words a precise cadence. "Anger makes strength, yes, but also weakness. We will work on this."

Matt leans closer to Hal. "You might remember him from the warehouse meetings."

Hal nods.

Claus inclines his head. "Not just fight. Live. Survive.

Learn when to strike and when to be silent." He gestures for Hal to follow him. "Come. We begin now."

Hal follows Claus to a secluded alcove of the cavern where a small underground stream creates a constant, soothing sound as it flows past. Lanterns cast a warm glow over the space, which has been set up with simple mats on the stone floor.

"Sit," Claus says, folding himself gracefully onto one of the mats.

Hal lowers his bulk awkwardly, the mat nearly disappearing beneath his mass. "I'm not sure meditation is what I need right now."

"You need everything right now," Claus says simply. "You are like a tree struck by lightning—burning, split open." His eyes take on a distant look. "I know this feeling. My Evan was killed at a AlignX protest march three years ago." His lips twist in bitterness. "As if love is disease."

"How do you live with it?" Hal asks.

"Not living with it—that is the wrong path," Claus corrects. "You transform it. Like ore into steel." He places his hands on his knees. "Now, we breathe."

The first session is agony for Hal. Sitting still while his mind replays the deaths of Mara and Brandon on an endless loop is torture. His body twitches with the need to move, to fight, to smash something. Claus watches with patient eyes.

"The body remembers what the mind wants to forget," Claus says. "Your enhancements make this harder. They are designed for action, not reflection."

Days pass. Each morning, Hal sits with Claus. Each session

stretches longer. Gradually, Hal learns to inhabit the moments between his breaths, to recognize the rage that surges through him not as an enemy to be fought but as energy to be channeled.

"Your enhancements are tools," Claus tells him. "Not you. The man who loves his son and wife, who would die to bring them back—that is you."

After a week of these sessions, Claus declares Hal ready for the next phase. They stand at the edge of the cave entrance, looking out at the densely wooded valley.

"We need a training ground," Claus says. "A place to prepare. Resistance members are brave but untrained. Many have never fought."

"You think there's going to be a war?" Hal squints against the morning light.

"I know there is," Claus replies. "People here are scared. Injured. Hungry. Most have lost someone. But there is still a long road ahead. It is imperative people have their eyes open. And it is imperative they are trained to fight."

Hal grits his teeth as the truth of Claus' words seep in. He hadn't thought much beyond Mara and Brandon, only about running through the woods. His rage had blinded him. But life continues. Hal has a future. One Mara wouldn't want him to throw away.

"Come." Claus gestures with his cane. "There's a meadow over that ridge. Surrounded by dense trees not visible from the air. I spotted it on my way here."

Hal nods. "Show me."

With Claus' limp, it takes them a little while to reach the ridge, especially as the older man refuses any help. Hal could pluck him off his feet and carry him, but Claus insists he needs to stay strong.

The meadow is perfect—a natural clearing ringed by towering pines that create both cover and obstacle.

"Here," Claus says, satisfaction in his voice. "We build here."

"Build?"

"A training course."

Over the next three days, Hal channels his grief into physical labor. It is far better than sitting in the cave and dwelling over his loss. He tucks that aside to deal with another time.

He moves fallen trees, creating natural barricades and obstacles. Claus directs the work with the precision of an architect, designing a training course that will challenge both enhanced and unmodified resistance members.

Other resistance fighters join them, bringing tools and supplies from the cave. Paige flies overhead, her green wings flashing in the sunlight as she keeps watch for patrols. Her aerial perspective helps them refine the layout.

"We need to simulate urban combat too," Hal says, hefting a massive log into position. "Most of the fighting will happen in cities, not forests."

Claus nods, stroking his mustache thoughtfully. "Yes. Buildings, doorways, confined spaces. Different tactics are needed."

Together, they create mock buildings using salvaged materials—fallen trees, stones, branches woven into walls.

By the third day, the training ground takes shape—a complex course of obstacles, hiding spots, climbing walls, and simulated urban environments. In the center, Claus creates a meditation circle.

"Balance," he explains. "Action and stillness. Attack and defense."

Hal stands at the edge of the meadow, surveying their work. It's not army training 101, but it's not far off.

"When do we start?" he asks.

Claus places a hand on Hal's armored shoulder. "We already have." He gestures to the setting sun filtering through the trees. "Tomorrow, we bring others. Tonight, one more lesson."

They sit in the center of the meadow as darkness falls, two silhouettes against the deepening blue of the sky.

"Remember why you fight," Claus says. "Not for revenge alone. Revenge burns fast, leaves ash. Fight for a world where no more children are taken, where choice remains sacred."

Hal closes his eyes, summoning the image of Brandon's face, of Mara's smile. "I'll try."

"Do not try," Claus says firmly. "Do. Or do not. There is no try."

Despite everything, Hal feels his lips twitch toward something resembling a smile. "Did you just quote a movie at me?"

For the first time, Claus' serious expression breaks into a small grin. "Wisdom comes from many sources. Even entertainment." His face grows solemn again. "But truth remains. Commitment must be complete. The path ahead is long."

As they walk back to the cave in the gathering darkness, Hal finally feels the importance of his bulk nanite. He was never meant for football. He was meant for war.

CHAPTER 9

THE TRAINING GROUND comes alive with the grunts and shouts of a few unadjusteds trialing the obstacle course. Hal watches from the center of the meadow. A week of working with Claus has transformed raw determination into disciplined purpose. He still wakes every morning with Brandon's name on his lips, still feels the phantom weight of his son in his arms, but the meditation techniques have given him ways to channel the grief rather than drown in it.

"Again," Hal calls to the group attempting to scale a twelve-foot wall he constructed from interlaced fallen trees. "Remember, in the city, you'll be climbing concrete and steel. This is the easy version."

Paige hovers above the wall, her green wings catching the light as she demonstrates the technique for those who can't fly. "Lead with your strongest side, find three points of contact before you move the fourth limb."

The whistle comes without warning—three sharp blasts, the signal for potential danger. Everyone freezes. Hal picks up the rapid approach of footsteps through the underbrush, heading toward the cave. Not the measured tread of military patrols, but something more urgent, less disciplined.

"Inside, now," Hal orders. The resistance fighters melt into the trees with practiced efficiency, moving toward the hidden cave entrance. The emergency drills were the first thing they practiced.

Francesca materializes at Hal's side, rifle in hand. "Two people coming from the east ravine," she says. "Matt's on lookout. Says one might be Silver."

Hal's pulse quickens. Silver Melody—the girl he's heard so much about but hasn't yet met. Matt's voice takes on a different quality whenever he mentions her, a softness that speaks volumes about his feelings.

"And the other?" Hal asks, already moving toward the cave.

Francesca's pace matches his longer strides. "Big. Matt thinks it might be another bulk."

"What about her father?"

"Unclear."

If they lose Rufus...they lose everything.

They reach the cave entrance just as a commotion erupts inside. Voices rise in surprise and welcome. Hal pushes through the gathered resistance members, and the crowd parts to reveal two newcomers standing in the cave's main chamber.

The girl must be Silver—tall, lithe, with dark hair and striking silver eyes that scan the room with quick intelligence. But it's her companion that stops Hal in his tracks.

"Joe?" The name escapes him in a disbelieving whisper.

Joe Rucker, all eight feet of him, turns at the sound of Hal's voice. His corn-colored hair is matted with dirt and what looks like dried blood, but his eyes light up when they land on Hal.

"Small!" Joe's booming voice echoes off the cave walls. "You made it!" He crosses the distance between them in three massive strides and engulfs Hal in a bear hug that would crush an unenhanced human. Against Hal's armored skin, it feels like coming home.

Joe steps back to look at his friend. His smile fades as he reads the grief etched in Hal's face. "Mara? Brandon?"

Hal shakes his head once, a jerky movement. "Gone."

Understanding passes between them. Joe squeezes his shoulder. "I'm sorry, man. So damn sorry."

For a moment, they're back on the field, the stadium lights bright overhead, the roar of the crowd a physical force pressing against them. Two bulks who found friendship in a world that saw them as commodities.

"How'd you get out?" Hal asks. "I tried to contact you, but cell service was jammed. Looks like you got the coordinates I sent though."

"I did," Joe replies. "That message saved my ass. As well as a certain young female."

It's only then Hal notices Joe isn't limping. He came to Central City to fight his case, and looks like he won in the best possible way.

Hal cocks his head. "She's got regeneration pills?"

Joe nods.

"That's a game changer."

"She's only got a handful."

Hal socks his shoulder. "And she gave one to you."

Joe grins and a blush lights up his cheeks.

"So it's like that?" Hal smiles, enjoying seeing Joe's discomfort.

"I don't know what you're talking about," Joe deadpans.

"Uh-huh," Hal laughs, then immediately feels guilty for the moment of revelry. It's too soon.

Silver approaches. Up close, Hal notices the tension around her eyes, the way she carries herself—alert, ready for anything. Matt hovers nearby, his expression wearing a medley of complicated emotions.

"Silver," Joe says, gesturing between them, "meet Hal Small. Best offensive lineman the Reapers ever had. Hal, this is Silver Melody."

"The scientist's daughter," Hal says, nodding.

A flash of something crosses Silver's face. "Yes. The scientist's daughter." Her voice is cool, assessing.

"Speaking of which...?" Hal probes.

Silver's expression hardens. "My dad was captured."

"That's how we met," Joe says.

"Joe saved me."

"And then you saved me." Joe bends his knee to indicate how well it's moving.

So no Rufus Melody. Shit. That means the resistance is on its own. Mostly unadjusteds, a few altereds against...President Bear's immortal army.

Hal swallows.

This doesn't change anything. It just makes it a little harder. That's all.

"We'll get him back," Hal tells Silver.

"Damn straight," she replies.

Hal studies Silver's face—the determination in her jaw, the intensity in her eyes. He recognizes that look. It's the same one he sees in a cracked piece of mirror each morning.

"What's the plan?" Hal asks.

Silver meets his gaze. "We break him out. Him and my mom."

"Your father can really reverse these enhancements?" Hal asks.

"He can," Silver replies. And that is all the motivation Hal needs.

He has nothing much to live for. He knows a fight against President Bear is a death wish, but he can't think of a better cause to risk his life for. Then he can be with Mara and Brandon again.

"Well, let's find out where they are," Hal says.

The End

If you want to know what happens to Hal once he meets up with Silver and team, don't forget to check out *The Unadjusteds*:

https://geni.us/Theunadjusteds

Read on for the first chapter in the next origin story, ***Kyle Lewis.***

If you want to experience more of my books, do join my Facebook readers group where you can chat to other readers and discuss my books, as well as anything else you are reading. I am very active in this group, and you can expect book jokes, puzzles, riddles, quizzes, giveaways, the opportunity to name characters, as well as secret information about what I'm working on, cover reveals and so much more!

Just click here: https://www.facebook.com/groups/840324970233576

Read on for the first chapter in the next origin story, ***Kyle Lewis.***

KYLE LEWIS

An Unadjusteds Story

MARISA NOELLE

He was built to be the poster boy of progress. But what if the future he's selling is a lie?

Kyle Lewis is fast—too fast. The youngest kid in Central City to receive a class 7 nanite, he's everything his parents and the government want him to be: a champion, an icon, the golden boy of the enhancement program. Cameras love him. Politicians need him. His parents control him.

But when Kyle witnesses the horrifying death of a classmate, and later discovers the hidden truth about the nanite system, his carefully constructed world shatters. Behind the glossy headlines and promises of evolution lies a system built on fear, control, and sacrifice. Torn between the legacy his family demands and the resistance calling for freedom, Kyle must decide who he really is—and what he's willing to risk.

Can one enhanced boy built to sell the system become the one to bring it down?

KYLE LEWIS

CHAPTER 1

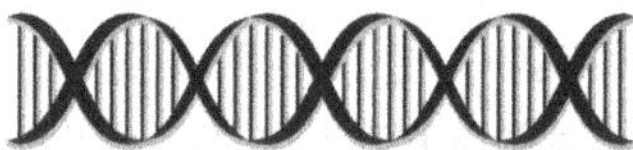

Kyle steps onto the mats, the world narrowing to the space between him and his opponent. He bounces on the balls of his feet, the hum of new energy vibrating through his muscles, whispering promises of victory. This is the last match of the day. The final. It all hinges on this moment.

His opponent stands opposite, a wall of muscle, sweat gleaming under the harsh arena lights. They circle. Kyle's pulse quickens. This is his first competition since taking the speed nanite.

The pill was delivered to him at a fancy catered dinner his Mom organized at home. Wrapped in a box with a ribbon. Speed isn't the obvious choice for karate, but Kyle wanted something different, something his opponents hadn't opted for, something that would give him an edge. There are no bulks in the karate circuit, yet. And Kyle didn't fancy being all jacked up and looking like he was juiced up on steroids, so speed it was. And it will give him an advantage against a bulk anyway.

He's spent the last week testing out his new limits. Grinning like a fool when he played out scenarios on EvolveMe. Smiling even harder when he took down opponents who didn't see him coming.

Claus, his sensei, has banned him from sparring with unadjusteds. Fair enough, Kyle reasons. Unadjusteds and altereds should never be pitted against each other. That's when things go wrong.

But now it's time to show the world what he's got. It's an important match. And he's the youngest person in the country to receive a Class 7 nanite. *Thanks Mom and Dad.* And also—no pressure.

He glances at Jax in the audience, his expression a complex mixture of admiration and determination. He's kitted out in the same dojo uniform as Kyle, but they won't be competing against each other. Jax hasn't taken a nanite. Yet.

Kyle notes the jealousy flickering through his best friend's eyes. Jax is taller, more muscular, maybe a better contender for a nanite. But Kyle got there first. On account of his dad being a spin doctor for the president and his mom being a nanite influencer with a gazillion followers. They didn't even have to pay for it.

He's lucky. He knows that. And if he could get Jax a nanite, he would. Hopefully his best friend will understand it's just a matter of time. Kyle has seen nanites tear more than one friendship apart. But that won't happen with him and Jax. They've known each other since kindergarten. Their moms are best friends. They're *bros.*

The referee signals. Kyle moves before the sound has fully left the whistle. His body reacts faster than thought, faster than instinct, faster than what should be humanly possible. *Sweet.* He launches toward his opponent, cursing himself for being too caught up in his own head just a moment ago, but that doesn't seem to matter now because he just dodged the first strike without trying.

He sidesteps a jab with such ease it feels like watching someone practice in slow motion, then counters with a flurry of strikes that connect before his opponent can blink. Each hit lands exactly where he wants it to, but it feels like he's beating up a practice dummy. This isn't skill alone anymore. This is something else. Something more. Something almost godly.

Kyle snaps his arm down in a fierce karate chop that smacks against his opponent's guard, the sound as sharp as the crack of splitting wood. The force drives his rival back a step, shock flashing across the boy's eyes, but he doesn't fall. Not yet.

His opponent lunges, muscles coiled like springs. To Kyle, it's laughable—every twitch of muscle, every bead of sweat flying from his brow happens at a crawl. Kyle weaves under a kick, grinning, a laugh bubbling up from his chest at the absurdity of it all.

This is so freaking cool!

He remembers when this boy used to beat him with his reflex nanites, back when Kyle's speed was human. Now, even enhanced reflexes look clumsy and predictable. The world stutters, dragging behind while Kyle races ahead.

The joy of it is undeniable. Each step, each dodge, each strike is a secret that belongs only to him. The crowd gasps, but Kyle hears it like a delayed echo, his body already moving on to the next motion, the next advantage. He could end the match at any moment, and the knowledge sends a thrill through him—tinged with a sliver of unease. If this is what one nanite can do, what happens when everyone takes one? What happens when speed isn't his gift anymore, but just another product in a bottle?

Then he catches her eye—Silver Melody, standing at the back of the bleachers. Her dark hair pulled into a messy knot, her silver eyes assessing. Her concern reaches him even from this distance.

His opponent scores a point against him. *Not cool.*

Kyle blinks, centers himself. *Focus,* he commands, thrusting away the internal debate. His opponent spins, an arc of fury aimed at Kyle's side. But Kyle is gone, moving with impossible speed, time bending around him. He strikes—a clean punch to the shoulder, sending his opponent spiraling down to the mats.

Something cracks, but the sound is covered by the erupting crowd. Noise floods his senses as medics rush toward the fallen rival, checking vitals, lifting him onto a stretcher. Kyle doesn't have the strength to hit someone hard enough to break a bone... but with added speed...? He never considered that possibility.

Crap.

Cheers wash over him in dizzying waves. Cameras flash. Smiles stretch.

Kyle pulls in a breath, finds his parents in the audience. They are beaming at him. Well, no, not at him. That's for the cameras. There are national network cameras here and his parents never miss an opportunity to increase their political reputation or follower counts. Since his mom got the turquoise eye-enhancing nanite, her following has doubled. It's become a family joke over the breakfast table when she logs on each morning to guess how many more she accrued overnight. Kyle always gets it wrong. Always underestimates. Never understands how many people love social media. Okay, yeah, he has his own following on EvolveME, but that's different. It's gaming. It's not jewelry and makeup and vacationing on an island.

Kyle leans down to his opponent before they wheel him away. He can't even remember his name. "Dude, I'm really sorry."

His opponent shrugs his good arm. "Don't worry about it. Nothing that a regen nanite won't fix."

The injured opponent is wheeled away. As well-wishers surround him, he's swept from the mats. He takes what feels like hours to fight his way through the crowds to the locker room, and by the time he gets there, he's exhausted.

The locker room is quieter than the arena, the echo of cheers replaced by the muffled hum of ventilation. Kyle sits on a bench, sweat cooling on his skin, hands still trembling with the aftershocks of speed. The adrenaline feels endless, like the nanite won't let him crash.

Claus finds him a couple of minutes later. He places a hand on Kyle's shoulder. "You fought well, Kyle-kun. *Yoku yatta." Well done.* His mouth curves into the faintest smile. "I am proud."

Kyle lets out a shaky laugh, the sound bouncing around the tiled walls. "Thanks, Sensei. I mean, did you see that? I was untouchable out there. Everything felt so... easy. Like I could see his moves before he even thought them."

Claus' expression doesn't change. "That is the danger." His voice is low. "*Jōnetsu wa chikara ni naru, shikashi yami ni mo naru.*" *Passion can become strength, but it can also become darkness.* He squeezes Kyle's shoulder, firm enough to ground him. "You are fast, faster than any man has a right to be. But karate is not about speed. It is about control. And balance."

Kyle swallows, the words subduing the high of his win. "I had control. Didn't I?"

Claus' gaze flickers to the mats visible through the open door, where sweat and blood still stains the floor. "Your fist says otherwise. You did not mean to hurt him, but intent and consequence do not always walk the same path. Never forget that."

Kyle nods, but the energy in his veins makes stillness impossible. He wants to move, to run, to fight again. He forces himself to meet Claus' eyes. "I'll be careful, Sensei."

Claus' voice softens. "Do not lose your head. You are a good boy, Kyle." He gets to his feet. "Remember—without discipline, speed is nothing but chaos."

Claus leaves him in the locker room to shower. Kyle has no more time to debate his conflicting feelings; his parents are waiting to take him to dinner. He goes through the motions of washing his hair and scrubbing his body, trying to pretend he doesn't hear the echo of the crunch of his opponent's shoulder breaking. But that is what regen nanites are for. They fix what's broken. And if you're going to play competitive sport, things are going to get broken.

Outside, Kyle finds the family car waiting for him. Harris

is in the driver's seat, hands on the steering wheel, white hat perched neatly on his head. It's a driverless car, but his parents like the ceremony of a driver. Said parents are in the back, both their faces lit up by their phone screens. They're laughing and smiling at each other, sharing bytes from their socials. No doubt about Kyle's dramatic win.

Harris spots Kyle, comes out of the car, and opens the door for Kyle to climb in.

Kyle slides into the leather seat, the door clicking shut behind him. His mother barely glances up from her phone before beaming at him, turquoise eyes shining with artificial brilliance. "Darling, you were incredible. The angles, the power—perfect for the highlight reels. My followers are already trending the clip." She squeezes his hand once, then turns her screen so Kyle can see a loop of his karate chop slowed down to cinematic perfection. The caption reads: *The Future of Sport—Kyle Lewis.*

His father leans forward, voice brimming with approval. "You showed control, son. Precision. Exactly what the program needs to see. I've already had two calls from officials wanting a statement. Tonight, you'll be the face of progress. Remember that." He pats Kyle's shoulder.

The car pulls away, Harris guiding it smoothly through the neon-lit streets of Central City. Digital billboards flash by, some already updated with Kyle's image mid-strike, his name bold beneath the NanoTech insignia.

His mother's laughter bubbles again as she scrolls, tilting her screen toward his father. "The Helix Lounge posted— they're reserving the crystal chamber just for us." She turns to Kyle, pride radiating from every polished pore. "Everyone will be there tonight, sweetheart. Politicians, influencers, sponsors. And all of them will want to meet *you*."

Kyle's not sure how he feels about that, but he nods and smiles just like he's expected to.

The candlelight in The Helix Lounge flickers over the polished tables, illuminating fine china and silver utensils. Kyle sits opposite his parents, scanning the menu, wondering when food started costing so much. But apparently their meal is *on the house,* and they can order *anything they like.* Kyle barely recognizes any of the words on the menu and asks the waiter to bring him something "simple." He's secretly hoping for a burger, not a holoshrimp cocktail or gene bean tartlets.

Their glasses are filled to the brim with champagne. Even Kyle's despite the fact he's only twelve.

"I'm so proud of you, son." His dad raises his glass.

The three of them clink, but Kyle doesn't sip before placing the crystal flute on the table.

His mom smiles. "You'll learn to love it."

"Maybe when I'm older."

His dad laughs and ruffles his hair. Like old times.

Kyle ducks under his hand and scans the seated guests, hoping no one noticed his dad being so embarrassing.

As they wait for their starters, his mom pushes her phone across the table. "Look. Sponsors are already offering. They saw how easily you won today, Kyle. You are the future of karate—"

"I'm nothing like Jacob Shea—"

His dad waves a dismissive hand. "He's older than you and he's taken a lot more nanites."

"Exactly," his mom agrees. "And there's no reason you

can't surpass his standard. With the right training. The right nanites. The right backing—"

Kyle throws up both hands, almost knocking his plate from the waiter's grasp. He's disappointed to see shells and cabbage and other things he can't identify. It does not look simple. "I thought I was just getting the speed nanite. I didn't think..." *It was going to become a whole thing.*

Both his parents frown.

"You can't stop at one," his dad says.

"You have to fight hard to stay at the top," his mom says.

As the waiter lays their food in front of them, Kyle gives his parents a once-over. Apart from his mom's turquoise eyes, there's nothing obviously altered about them. But he knows they've both taken numerous nanites. Lesser ones that help them with their careers. Kyle gave up counting the packets that came through the doors a couple of years ago. At least they haven't opted for antlers or bunny tails. *Jeez.*

Not that he has anything against anyone who does choose those. Each to their own and all that. It's just not right for Kyle.

The waiter leaves.

"Anyway," his mom says, pointing at her phone. "There is more than one nanite to help you on the mat." She scrolls through endless streams of Class 6 and Class 7 nanite choices. The options start to blur in Kyle's head. Her murmurs rise over the din of the restaurant, discussing the merits of enhanced reflexes and teleportation, as if shopping for clothes.

"This could guarantee your future edge," she says, eyes not lifting from the list, food untouched.

His dad echoes her sentiment with his spin-doctor vocabulary. "We'll invest in anything that cements your lead."

Kyle nudges a shell with his fork. He thinks it's a snail. They're going through a French phase at The Helix Lounge. All he wants is a burger and a chocolate shake.

His thoughts tumble. His stomach growls. His parents urge him to dig in. The match plays in his mind, as well as the crack of breaking bone.

To carry on reading, click here:
https://geni.us/KyleLewis